PARANORMAL COZY MYSTERY

Tattoos & Clues

TRIXIE SILVERTALE

Sittin' On A Goldmine
Productions L.L.C.

Sittin' On A Goldmine Productions, L.L.C.

pr@sittinonagoldmine.co

www.sittinonagoldmine.co

This is a work of fiction. Names, characters, places, and incidents are products of the author's imagination or are used fictitiously and are not to be construed as real. Any resemblance to actual events, locales, business establishments, organizations, or persons, living or dead, is entirely coincidental.

ISBN: 978-0-9998758-7-2

Cover Design © Sittin' On A Goldmine Productions, L.L.C.

Trixie Silvertale
Tattoos and Clues: Paranormal Cozy Mystery : a novel / by
Trixie Silvertale — 1st ed.

[1. Paranormal Cozy Mystery — Fiction. 2. Cozy Mystery — Fiction. 3. Amateur Sleuths — Fiction. 4. Female Sleuth — Fiction. 5. Wit and Humor — Fiction.] 1. Title.

CHAPTER 1

As I DRIFT between the luscious memory of dreams and the insistent arrival of reality, a large paw thwaps my forehead. A moment too late, I recognize the rough caress of my dearly departed grandmother's fiendish feline.

I roll my head to the left, but the lightning reflexes of the rescued caracal are a step ahead.

His fangs give my tender ear a nip.

My hands press against his tan fur to retaliate with a shove to the floor, but the thick scar behind his scapula fills my heart with forgiveness. He took a bullet for me—and my dad. I guess he can bite my earlobe.

It's still hard to believe how my life changed with the contents of one manila envelope. I went from poor orphaned barista, living in a run-down studio apartment in Sedona, Arizona to wealthy bookshop owner, with a father, in the quaint town of Pin Cherry Harbor. Plus I have this cat . . .

I scratch his head right between his black tufted ears, and his purring shakes the whole bed. "All right, Pyewacket, I'll feed you."

As I rise from the soft, fluffy pillow and push back the cozy down comforter, I can't protect my heart from the shock of what my sleepy grey eyes behold.

Let me assure you I'm not referring to the large caracal that slobbered in my ear.

Nope. Turns out, I'm not alone in my antique four-poster bed.

Next to me, painted in dappled autumn sunlight, lies a man.

This man is handsome. His hair is a tousled mess of buttery brown and his chin whispers of stubble. His T-shirt and jeans adorn my floor. His name is lost.

Pyewacket fixes me with a judgmental stare and casually cleans one of his tufted ears with a dangerously clawed paw.

This guy's name is somewhere in my rum-logged brain. Greg? Larry? Gilligan? Oh, come on, Moon! You certainly didn't bring the Skipper's little buddy home. "Gary!" I did not mean to shout that at the top of my lungs.

The man next to me rockets up and one hand dives beneath his pillow. "What happened?" he stammers in a husky voice.

I play coy. "What do you mean? Are you okay?"

He catches sight of Pye and hastily dives out of the bed. "What the—?"

"That is Pyewacket. He was my—" Before another word passes my lips, I search the air for any sign of my grandmother's strangely absent ghost. She probably didn't leave me a gorgeous three-story bookshop and this swanky apartment for one-night hookups with dockworkers I pick up at the Final Destination dive bar, but I'm still adjusting to small-town life in almost-Canada. "Pye was my late grandmother's cat."

He shakes his head and keeps his stare fixed on the caracal as he backs toward his pile of clothes. "That ain't no cat. That's a lion." Gary dresses faster than any fling in recent memory and looks around the room in confusion. "How the heck did we get in here?"

Pyewacket leaps off the bed with an effortless push of his powerful hind legs and looks toward the secret door.

I still don't sense the otherworldly presence of Grams anywhere. Bonus points for me if I can keep it that way. "Don't worry. I have to feed the cat. I'll show you out."

As I slip out of bed, Pye crouches low and slinks toward the already shaky Gary.

He fumbles around in his pockets and scans the floor.

"Did you lose something?" I ask, nonchalantly.

A low growl emanates from Pyewacket, and Gary backs away as he replies, "Yeah, I can't find my . . . phone." His eyes dart and his fists clench.

Even my pickled brain can pick up on the fact that he's lying. To be clear, it could be my gift of clairsentience functioning despite my hangover, but I barely know what the word means—let alone how the gift technically works.

Glancing down to make sure my bits are covered, I laugh at the phrase on my oversized tee. "I Drink and I Know Things." One thing I clearly don't know is when to stop drinking. I fluff my extra-messy, snow-white hair and shuffle toward the hidden exit.

Gary follows me hesitantly toward the wall, which I know is a secret door from my apartment to the bookshop. Unfortunately, the sexy-but-not-too-bright Gary is confused by the lack of a traditional door—and also terrified that my giant cat is going to eat him.

He looks left and right. "Hey man, joke's over. Let me outta here, okay? Last night was great. You're great. I'll call you—"

Gary is a delicious conundrum. The typical fare of my previous life in Arizona, and a leftover bad habit in a new town. He is hunky, muscular, tall-ish, and jerk-adjacent. I will not let this bad decision escape without amusing myself. "Just say my name and you'll be out in a flash."

The utter blankness of his stare would be comical if it weren't so insulting.

"Courtney?" he whispers.

"Not even close," I mumble as I walk toward my fully stocked walk-in closet.

He shouts a series of equally incorrect names at my back.

I enter the closet, jump at the glowering stare of my hovering Grams, and grab what I need.

"We'll be discussing this later, young lady," Isadora announces as she crosses her bejeweled limbs over her vintage Marchesa silk-and-tulle burial gown.

Fortunately, I'm the only one who is tuned into her ghostly frequency.

I return to the main room to find that Pye has my "rando" cornered and there are little beads of perspiration on Gary's full upper lip.

"I'm going to have to put this blindfold on you, Gary. I hope you understand." As I approach, he bristles.

"No way. No way are you putting that thing on me." He squares his shoulders and clenches his jaw.

I step closer to the ready-to-pounce Pye and coo softly, "This guy doesn't want you to get your breakfast. What do you think about that?"

The magnificent Pyewacket arches his back, raises his hackles, and replies, "RE-OW!"

Pretending to shudder, I say, "Oh, that does not sound good Gary." I ponder my next move when—

A stern voice crackles over the intercom. "I saw a strange van parked outside, Mitzy. I'm comin' up."

I've never been so happy to hear my father's voice. Well, maybe *never* is too strong a word since we haven't known each other that long, but I'm extremely pleased at his over-protective instincts right now.

The secret wall/door slides open and the menacing frame of my six-foot-and-change ex-con father, topped with a shock of white-blonde hair like my own, fills the large gap. "You know this guy?" snarls Jacob.

I shrug. "He was just leaving. Pye and I were having a little fun." I dangle the blindfold.

My dad, quick to read a room, doesn't miss a beat. "You get dressed. I'll take out the trash."

He grabs Gary by the scruff of the neck and steers him out of the apartment.

"HISS." Pyewacket wishes Gary a hasty retreat.

"Eyes front," growls my dad.

Gary whimpers.

Rapid footfalls descend the iron spiral staircase to the first floor and the heavy metal door leading into the alley slams shut with finality.

A smug grin spreads from ear to ear as I turn to search for my jeans.

"Not so fast, hussy."

Uh oh. Ghost-ma is on the rampage.

"And give me one good reason I shouldn't be angry with you, Mizithra Achelois Moon."

"We agreed that you wouldn't read my thoughts, Grams." It's a feeble comeback.

"Well, let's also agree that all bets are off when you bring men of questionable motives into our sanctuary!"

I open my mouth to protest, but she has a solid point.

"You have hundreds of rare books in that store, priceless family heirlooms in this apartment, and, most importantly—your precious heart." A ghostly tear trickles down her timeless face.

"You couldn't be more right. I wasn't thinking straight. I was feeling sorry for myself because there's nothing to do and I went to that stupid bar next to the train depot . . . I drank too much rum."

"I know a way to stop that." Grams crosses her arms and arches a perfectly drawn brow.

"Just because you were in AA, Grams, doesn't mean everyone is an alcoholic."

"We're not talking about everyone, Mitzy. We're talking about you." Grams freeze-frames for a moment and vanishes.

"Grams? Grams, don't leave like that."

Jacob re-enters in time to hear my last words. "You and Mom fighting?" he asks.

"She's upset that I brought that guy back here and thinks I should go to AA."

He sighs and shakes his head. "She's not wrong."

"What? You think I'm an alcoholic, too?"

He walks toward me and opens his arms. "I'm in no position to judge you, sweetie, but that guy was hiding something. No decent guy drives around in a van with a bed in the back and 'Waterbeds Unlimited' emblazoned on the side."

Unsavory images of last night's drunken escapades dance through my mind. I shiver and slip into my dad's waiting hug. But before I can make any apologies or promises, Grams materializes beside the bed and says a single word that turns my blood to ice.

"Gun."

My whole body stiffens.

Jacob leans back. "What's wrong?"

I keep forgetting I'm the only one who can see

and hear my dearly departed matriarch. "Grams is over there." I gesture to the left side of the bed, between the heavily draped six-by-six windows and the tiger-maple nightstand. "She said 'gun.'"

Jacob's arms fall to his sides and he walks toward the ghost he can't see. "Ask her where."

Grams points to the left finial. "It's under the bed. Between this post and the wall."

"Behind the left leg," I relay.

My dad drops to the floor, shimmies under the bed, and stands up holding a black pistol. He drops it on the bed and uses the edge of a sheet to wipe it clean.

"Dad?"

"Sorry," he whispers. "Force of habit."

I walk to the bed and glance down at the firearm. "That's not mine."

"Probably safe to assume it's Gary's."

"He was definitely looking for something this morning, and it wasn't seconds." I'm a heartbeat too late in realizing that this is not the audience for that joke. But as I recall the way Gary's hand dove under his pillow—

Ghost-ma gasps.

Another thoughtless intrusion into my private musings.

Dad is stoic.

"He works down at the docks. It's probably for protection," I offer lamely.

"It's definitely for protection, Mitzy. But what does he need protection from in Pin Cherry Harbor?" Jacob shakes his head and adds, "The only gang around here is Ethel and her bingo gals down at the Elks' Lodge."

Grams chuckles in spite of the tension.

I glance at the gun and suspicions flood my hungover brain.

Grams clears her throat.

I put up a hand and shake my head. "Dad, I need to get dressed—"

"Ree-ow." A gentle reminder.

"And feed Pye. Why don't I meet you at the diner in twenty minutes and we can discuss Gary and that gun." I gesture to the pistol.

Jacob steps away from the weapon and nods slowly. "When you hand that off to the sheriff, don't mention my name."

"Of course."

He hurries out without a backward glance. Shoulders hunched. Jaw clenched.

"See you in a few," I call as the bookcase door slides shut.

I rub my forehead and stumble to the bathroom. Placing two hands on the marble vanity, I stare into the antique mirror. Things may be strange, but they could be worse. When I did a runner on my previous life and took "Dante's" bus from Arizona to a place north of north, I wasn't exactly leaving a success story in my wake.

"Ree-OW!" A warning punctuated by a threat.

Time to feed the beast, or risk losing a finger.

A firm push of the small decorative plaster panel above the intercom opens the secret door from my apartment to reveal the second floor of my bookshop. I walk out onto the Rare Books mezzanine and Pye whips past, knocking me sideways in his haste to get downstairs.

Sliding my hand down the wrought-iron railing to keep myself upright, I circle down the spiral staircase to the thick carpet on the main floor.

Pye wraps himself between my feet in figure eights as soon as I reach the back room. "It's happening. Simmer down." I grab a bowl and dump a large portion of Fruity Puffs into the vessel.

Pye lifts up on his hind legs and nearly tips the bowl from my hands with his thick skull.

"Here. Here." I set the bowl down and step away. I made the mistake of attempting a friendly scratch on the back during his breakfast—once.

I push "brew" on the coffeemaker and plunk myself into a straight-backed wooden chair.

"Any plans today, dear?"

I gasp and exhale loudly. "Myrtle Isadora Johnson Linder Duncan Willamet Rogers!"

Grams giggles.

Her ghost is tethered to my bookshop, the Bell, Book & Candle, and she makes a habit of scaring the bejeezus out of me with unannounced pop-ins.

"I'll do the sparkly fade-in thing next time. I promise." She clutches at her strings of pearls and curtsies elegantly in her gown.

"You're too much." I pour my java, bravely add some past-the-expiration-date cream, and return to my slumped posture in the chair.

Pye sits back and begins his morning ritual of paw, face, and whisker cleaning, which reminds me it's been a few days since my last shower.

"Ghosts can't smell, sweetie."

I roll my eyes in exasperation. "Grams, my lips have to be moving, all right?"

"Of course. It's so easy to get confused, you know. Everything comes through on the same wavelength and it seems as though it is out loud, so—"

I point a firm finger toward my lips.

"Yes, dear, I'll watch for moving lips." She swirls toward Pyewacket and runs her ghost fingers along his back.

His tufted ears twist like cat satellite dishes, but he's growing accustomed to these energetic exchanges and he purrs softly.

"Time to get dressed and head down to the diner. Dad won't wait too long for breakfast." No sooner do I rise from the chair than Pye prowls over to the metal door leading to the alleyway and rakes his claws down the well-scratched paint.

"He wants to go out." Grams smiles at the creature that used to belong to her and nods like a proud parent.

When I open the door, he drops his rump firmly on my foot and does not budge.

"In or out, Pye?" A crisp autumn wind whistles through the cracked opening.

He is still as a stone statue.

"Come on, Pye. I need to go get human breakfast." I shiver uncontrollably.

He appears to have grown roots into the floor.

I let the door slam shut. "Suit yourself."

Leaving him to his stubbornness, I walk back to the elegant circular staircase.

Tan fur flies past me, and Pye takes up a defensive stance on the fourth stair.

"Uh, Grams? What the heck is going on?"

"Well, I used to take him for walks along the lakeshore. He probably wants you to go outside with him."

"A cat who needs a walker?" I put a foot on the bottom step.

Pye growls softly.

"Pye if I take you for a short walk, will you let me go and get breakfast?"

He shakes his hackles down and prances up the stairs.

I wag my head and approach the wall-mounted candle that must be tipped down to activate the mechanism which slides open the bookcase revealing my plush apartment.

Grams vanishes into the wall and I catch up to her in the glorious *Sex and the City* meets *Shopaholics* closet, which is larger than my entire previous crappy apartment.

"There's a whole section of lovely yoga pants, leggings, and tank tops over there." Grams points to a series of built-in drawers.

I open a drawer to reveal more fashionable workout gear than I could wear in a year—if I actually worked out. I pull out random pieces and admire them. "Grams, you were sixty-five when you died, and you said that you'd been ill for over a year, right?"

"That's right, dear. It was hard on Odell, but he was by my side until the end."

My question has nothing to do with her laundry list of ex-husbands. "What I'm getting at is the hip-factor in this closet. I get the vintage couture—you had money and you bought whatever you liked, but this drawer full of too-hot-for-Bikrams workout gear doesn't seem like your style."

A ghostly giggle flutters through the hallowed fabrics.

I look up and give my Ghost-ma a suspicious glare.

"Truth time?" she asks.

"We say, 'keepin' it a 100.' But whatever you want to call it, this closet just became your confessional." Hands on hips, I wait.

"When I told my lawyer that I wanted to change my will and leave everything to you, he encouraged me to buy you all the gifts I'd wanted to give you during those years your father forbade the family from contacting you—when he thought you were better off not knowing about him."

My arms slip to my sides. "You mean grumpy old Silas Willoughby told you to buy indulgent presents for a granddaughter you'd never meet?" I could not picture that hound-dog-cheeked man encouraging such extravagance.

She shrugs and floats to the far corner near the floor-to-ceiling shoe racks.

"Grams?"

"Well, after he'd been reading in one of the books about a way to keep a soul from crossing over . . ." She nods and grins sheepishly.

"So you're well and truly stuck here? It's not one of those unfinished-business kind of things?"

"I'm pretty sure I can stay forever, dear. Are you upset with me?"

"Upset? Are you kidding? I spent the last ten years thinking I was an orphan, and now I have a grandmother—and a dad."

"REE-ow!" The sound of imminent retribution.

"Oh, dear! You best take Pyewacket on that walk before he does something drastic."

I quickly don a pair of seriously punk-rock pocket leggings, a side-cinch tank, and a thick hooded cardigan. I fire off a quick text to my dad and force my phone into the tight little pocket on the thigh.

Grams swirls toward a pair of lightweight hiking shoes . . . and before Pye can cause me any harm, I'm ready.

This time when I open the side door into the alley, a blur of tawny fur and black tufts shoots past me without hesitation.

A brisk wind blows across the lake and howls between the buildings as I hurry toward the low wall that dead ends the backstreet.

Pye leaps five or six feet in the air, heaves his powerful back legs against the dumpster, and sails over the wall with ease.

I kick, push, and struggle to lift myself up and over the four-foot barrier.

Once I brush off the debris and straighten my sweater I catch the flash of sunlight, dancing across the waves. I have to remind myself that I'm looking at a massive freshwater lake and not an ocean, but the way the surf is crashing on the shore, that's a tough sell.

Pye is deftly leaping from one boulder to the next and heading toward a raised rocky outcrop.

I zip up against the stiff breeze and add a plucky little pep to my step with a jog toward the promontory. The terrain dips down before it rises back up to the berm that separates the sand and rocks from the dune grass. As I crest the hill, the muscular Pyewacket is crouched low, inching over the boulders in extreme stealth mode.

By the power of Grayskull! I do not want to see a rabbit or seabird murdered before my breakfast. I run toward the fiend making as much noise as possible. "Run little bunny or whatever you are! Flee before death becomes you!" I flap my arms and create a general nuisance of myself.

Pye freezes and only the tip of his oddly short tail twitches.

I rush up behind him, screech to a halt, and throw up a little bit in my mouth.

CHAPTER 2

SPINNING AWAY from the horrible sight, I wiggle my hands in the "oh that is ookey" dance while gulping in fresh air. My insides turn cold, I can't lift my arms, and my stomach is performing a pre-heave churn.

As I struggle and fail to extract my phone from the overly snug pocket on the leggings, movement on the road catches my eye. Hooray! A patrol car cruising along First Avenue.

It takes all of my strength to force my arms into the air. I wave my hands helplessly and jump up and down.

Tires screech.

Lights flash.

A car door slams.

My eyes widen and my tummy tingles—in the

yummy way. If this were one of my student films, I'd tell the camera operator to push-in and get every detail of this arrival.

Sheriff Erick Harper walks toward me in the finest pair of well-worn blue jeans I've ever inspected. And I am inspecting the crap out of these.

He waves.

I close my gaping jaw and try not to stare at the T-shirt that is straining to contain his well-defined pecs under a brown leather bomber jacket.

He smooths back his loose blonde bangs and nods. "What's going on, Moon? Why'd you wave me down?"

Oh, right. The thing . . .

Pye chooses that moment to growl fiercely.

"Hey, I told your grandmother and I'll tell you the same, you can't have that wild critter running loose. You have to put him on a leash."

Unable to contain my scoff, I reply, "Pyewacket? On a leash? You can't be even a little bit serious, Erick?"

"I've asked you to call me Sheriff Harper, Miss Moon." He smiles a little, but tilts his head as though he's scolding a small child.

Which instantly triggers my intense dislike of condescension. "How's that workin' out for ya?"

He shakes his head and walks toward me. "Now, what's this all about?"

I cover my mouth with one hand and gesture to the rocks with the other.

He looks back and forth. "These rocks? I know they look a bit strange, but the locals call this Boiler-plate Beach because of the way the water shaped—"

"Not the rocks! That!" I interrupt his geology lesson and make an "up and over" motion to indicate something on the other side of the rocks.

He climbs higher and looks down.

His hand goes for his radio. But he's in civilian clothes—such lovely, perfect civilian clothes—and there is no radio.

"Maybe call it in from the car?" I suggest.

He turns and eyes me in a way that is both insulting and also arousing.

"You're not going to accuse me of murder again are you?" I stick my hands on my hips.

He shakes his head. "You do seem to be some kind of magnet for corpses."

"Rude!"

He chuckles. "Why don't you tell me how you managed to find this one?"

His smile kinda melts my insides.

"I'll grab my notebook from the car. Don't go anywhere, all right?"

"Yes, Sheriff. I promise not to leave town." I roll my eyes for emphasis, in case he misses the sarcasm.

He takes off in a quick jog, and a grin slinks

across my face as I forget all about feeling insulted. When he returns, I tell my tale. But we'll skip ahead since you were there.

". . . So I walked up to see what Pye was stalking and—" I cover my mouth and shiver. "It's soggy, and swollen, and maybe a little scorched?" There is definitely something roiling violently in my gut.

"That'll do, Moon. Definitely looks like a drowning, but I can't account for the burning you ment—" He closes his note pad and leans toward me. "You all right?"

His concern is swoon-worthy. Or maybe I'm—

Strong arms catch me and guide me down the hill, away from the "finding."

Pyewacket growls once before he leaps from the mound and races back toward the bookshop.

"Coward," I mumble.

Erick pats my shoulder mechanically. "You're no coward, Miss Moon. I did two tours in Afghanistan and I've been in law enforcement for almost six years—still unsettles me."

The deep emotion in his voice, combined with his physical nearness, threatens to topple me a second time. "I'm fine. I just haven't eaten any breakfast."

"I'd drop you at Myrtle's Diner, but I have to wait for the medical examiner. Is there someone you can call?"

After ten years spent believing I was an orphan, my knee-jerk thought is "no." But I'm not an orphan. I have a dad. A living, breathing father. "I can call my dad," I say with a foolish grin.

Erick nods.

The industrial-strength fabric of the stretchy yoga pants refuses to cooperate and no matter how hard I battle, I can't seem to extract my phone.

A low chuckle fills the early-morning quiet. "I'll call him."

Before I can respond, Erick phones Jacob and tattles on me.

I wave my hand frantically. "Give me the phone."

His eyes twinkle as he passes it over with a warning, "Make it short. This is an active crime scene."

My eyelids squeeze to slits and I glare. "Yes, Sheriff." I snatch the phone. "Dad? Yeah, totally fine. I just found the thing wedged in the . . . I don't want to talk about it . . . No, I can walk . . . Sure. Ten minutes sounds great . . . All right. Bye" I pass the mobile back to Erick.

With the cell in one hand, he helps me to my feet with the other. "Are you sure you can make it to the diner?"

The wooziness is gone. Irritation is quickly replacing it. "I felt a little light-headed, I'm not a basket case."

He raises his hands in surrender and backs away. "I'm sure you understand the importance of keeping a lid on this ongoing investigation, right?"

I tilt my head and purse my lips. "You know this town better than me, Erick. Tally will probably tell me about this before I can place my order."

Pumping up the stern official-ness of his gaze, he adds, "I'd appreciate it if you don't pour fuel on the fire."

A sudden thought strikes. "You grew up around here, right? I mean, you pretty much know everyone. Did you recognize—it? Wasn't there a tattoo on the arm?" My brain is calling up the image my tummy does not want to review.

He grins. "You better get to breakfast, Miss Moon. And I recommend you leave this to the professionals. Understood?"

I nod in a completely noncommittal way and hurry off toward the diner. I can be very professional. He'll see.

The sight of Myrtle's Diner warms my heart and shifts my restless stomach to a more acceptable rumble of hunger. As I push open the door, Jacob slides out of the booth and meets me in two large strides.

Strong arms encircle me, and my father's reassuring voice whispers, "It's a little odd to hear your voice on Erick's phone—first thing in the morning. If I hadn't just ushered Gary out of your place, I might think there's something you're not telling me about your relationship with Sheriff Harper." He chuckles.

Basking in the moment of parental concern, I allow myself to entertain the idea. The truth? I wish there was something I wasn't telling him. Sadly my unrequited longing for Sheriff Too Hot To Handle is still the best-kept secret in Pin Cherry Harbor. And trust me, keeping a secret in this podunk town is a real feat!

I hardly have a chance to slide my eighty-eight percent polyester covered bottom into the booth before Tally sets a mug of steaming-hot coffee on the table.

"Morning, Mitzy." She smiles and nods.

"Good morning, Tally. How's your daughter?" I slip my hands around the ample mug.

Tally bobs her head a few times but her flame-red bun remains firmly perched on top of her head. "Well, she's right as rain and twice as welcome. I don't know how I'd make it through the weekend rushes without her."

"Good to hear. We'll have two specials." I smile as the older woman scurries off to the kitchen, and I glance back toward the cook.

Odell Johnson, my grandmother's first husband, gives me a friendly salute with his spatula through the orders-up window.

Dad slides the sugar toward me and I push it straight back. "Cream only."

He smiles and chuckles. "I'll add that to 'doesn't share fries.' I'm learning all your secrets." He returns the sugar to the wire holder at the end of the table and fixes me with a fatherly stare. "So, what happened out at Boilerplate this morning?"

I shake my head sternly. "Not only was I warned to keep my mouth shut by our bossy local sheriff—and there's nothing going on there, by the way—but I also do not want to talk about that on an empty stomach." My tummy twirls in warning.

Jacob leans back against the red vinyl-covered bench seat. "Maybe you should move out to the estate with me. You seem to attract trouble, and I'd like to be able to take better care of you." He breaks eye contact. "Make up for lost time, you know?"

Both of us wish we could get back the years he spent in prison and all the years before that, when he didn't know I existed. But all we have is now. My mom had a one-night stand, she ended up pregnant and never told the guy—cut to Grams' Last Will and Testament and me escaping my old life to unexpectedly find a family in Pin Cherry.

The phone on the wall rings and disrupts my reverie.

Jacob stiffens and lays both hands flat against the silver-flecked white table. He exhales slowly through his nose.

My super senses spark, and I feel Jacob's fear as strongly as if it were my own. "What's wrong, Dad?"

"Bells. Alarms." He leans back and sighs. "It's a prison thing."

I nod and sense the emotion fade. But the lull is short lived.

Tally answers and mumbles, "Right away." She looks at me as she hangs the receiver in the cradle.

My chest constricts.

She disappears into the back and reappears followed by the sheriff. Tally shakes her head and rushes out of the kitchen, looking pale and worried.

I can't tear my eyes from the silent movie playing out through the orders-up window.

Erick approaches Odell at the griddle and puts a hand on his shoulder.

Odell turns toward the visitor and his lined face transforms from crusty, old diner-owner to broken-hearted man in the space of thirty seconds. He steps away from the cooktop, nods to the sheriff, and takes a moment to collect himself as Erick slips out the back exit.

I'm frozen in mid-sip of coffee when Odell turns and locks eyes with me.

Pain grips his face and his eyes glisten with unshed tears. He swallows and walks out of the kitchen in a straight line toward our table.

I set my cup down. He knows the victim. I recognize that anguish on his face, or do I feel it in my bones? It's the same ache that gripped me for years after the news of my mother's fatal accident was delivered by my babysitter. "Can I get you—?"

Tally hands him the glass of water I gladly would've retrieved.

He waves it away and places both hands on the edge of our worn table. "I'm going to need your help, Mitzy."

"Of course. I'll do whatever I can, but what do you need?"

"That body you found—" His voice breaks and he lifts a hand to keep us quiet while he struggles for composure. "That was my little brother."

CHAPTER 3

My father and I exchange pained glances and fall silent as Odell explains how the medical examiner used to book private guided fishing tours on one of Walt's boats every summer. "He knew it was Walt as soon as he saw the tattoo."

"The mermaid?"

Odell stiffens and mumbles, "You saw it?"

"Only for a second. Then I flagged down the police car." I reach out and place my hand tentatively on top of Odell's fist, hardened by decades of work. "I'm so sorry. I'm so very sorry." I glance up at my father.

Jacob shakes his head. "Walter was a good man, Odell. He'll be missed."

I pat the gnarled knuckles and add, "I wish I could've known him. What can I do, Odell?"

He swallows once and coughs to clear his throat. "Walt had some struggles these last few years. Sheriff says they're treating this as suspicious circumstances but they haven't ruled out suicide." He gestures toward my father. "You found evidence the cops missed on his case, so I figure I'd get you to poke around and see who done Walt in—"

"I'm no—"

Odell again lifts his hand to shush me. "Walt was a lot of things, but he ain't the type to kill himself. Somebody is gonna pay for this, and I'm bettin' you're my best shot at getting to the truth."

I look at my dad, back to Odell and shrug. "So, you're hiring me?"

A hint of a smile tugs at the corner of Odell's downturned mouth. "I already got you on the 'free burgers for life' plan. I was hoping you'd consider that a down payment."

I squeeze his hand. "Of course. I'd do it for free. I'm just making sure I have my story straight for Erick. I mean, Sheriff Harper."

Odell and Jacob exchange a glance I don't appreciate.

"What?" I force my face into a mask of innocence. "He told me to leave it to the professionals, so—"

"Professionals," my dad says with a scoff. "Lotta good that did me."

Tally nudges Odell out of the way and lays two plates on the table. Mine contains scrambled eggs with chorizo and jalapeños, a heap of home fries, and one strip of bacon. Jacob's "special" consists of two massive blueberry pancakes and four sausages.

Odell inspects the order and nods his approval.

I still don't understand how he knows exactly what folks want for breakfast, but I suppose after running a diner for nearly half a century, some things are second nature.

"I'll let you dig in, but come round later and I'll fill you in about Walt." He raps his knuckles on the table and returns to the kitchen.

Jacob and I eat in silence. With grub this good in front of me, I tend to stay focused.

I finally set my fork down and lean back.

My dad wipes a little syrup from the corner of his mouth and grins. "I don't want you getting yourself into any hot water with the sheriff."

An image of Erick and me lounging in a hot tub flashes through my mind. I imagine what his chiseled chest must look like under that tight tee he wore this morning.

"A father might be concerned about a smirk like that."

I wipe all expression from my face. Somehow I had allowed the lascivious grin to slip from my mind to my mouth. Oops. "I'm always in trouble with the law around here. Seems they don't like out-siders or newcomers."

My dad raises one eyebrow. "Trust me, they're not real fond of convicts-come-home either."

My dad robbed a big box store and did some hard time. There, we've got that out of the way. He's reformed and we're figuring out how to build some kind of relationship after twenty-one years of my life spent thinking he either hated me or might be dead.

He pushes his plate back. "I have a meeting with Cal's attorney. I guess she's actually my at-torney now . . ."

A quiet sadness settles over him and he sips the last of his coffee.

"I'm sorry you didn't get a chance to talk things over with your father before he was—before he passed away." I stumble over the polite way to dis-cuss my grandfather's murder and sigh in frus-tration.

A hopeful light brightens Jacob's grey eyes. "Maybe he'll become a ghost like Isadora?"

"According to Grams, that's not how it works. But what do I know? I have exactly one case study to draw from."

He nods. "I'll catch up with you later. You'll be at the bookshop?" He slides out of the booth.

"Yeah, Twiggy wants to go over inventory, then

I'm back here to meet with Odell, but we could grab supper somewhere."

"Why don't you come out to the estate and we'll take the boat over to Chez Osprey before they close the island for the season."

"Sounds fancy."

"Is that a bad thing?" Jacob tilts his head.

I shrug. "I'm not used to fancy. Back in Sedona I reused my coffee grounds until the filter ripped or the brew looked like weak tea. I took a mostly cold shower three times a week and washed my clothes by hand in the bathroom sink."

He chuckles. "Preaching to the choir, Mitzy. I might've been raised with money, but after Cal cut me off and I ended up in prison . . . Well, coming back into all this is kinda throwing me off balance. But I don't want to take you out there because it's fancy. I want to show you the Osprey because it was your grandmother's favorite place. Not just the restaurant—the island was special to her."

I reach into my pocket to pay the bill, but my dad beats me to the punch and lays a fifty dollar bill on the table. I open my mouth to protest.

"I have a lot of father-daughter moments to make up for, honey. Let's agree that you'll never pay for a meal in my presence. Give your old man that much, all right."

"All right." I stretch out the hem of my tank top

and feign a curtsy. "What time should I be at the manse?"

"Manse?" Jacob screws up his face in confusion.

"Short for mansion."

No response.

"I was just trying it out."

He laughs. "Come out as early as you can. That way we can take our time out on the lake."

"I'll try, but Grams will want me to get all dolled up. You know she filled a closet with clothes for me before she even knew me?"

A pained expression washes over my dad's face. "It was selfish of me to forbid the family from contacting you. I thought your life would be better without a convict dad, but Isadora and Cal would've done right by you." He sighs. "I can't go back in time, but I'll do my best to make it up to you."

"All we have is today, right?"

"Right." He puts a strong arm around my shoulders and gives me a squeeze. "See you later—at the manse." His strong shoulders shake with laughter as he exits the diner.

CHAPTER 4

WALKING BACK DOWN MAIN STREET, toward the
bookshop, I soak in the view of the sun-drenched
great lake. How much longer can this gorgeous autumn weather hold? The locals always talk about
the storm of 19-something-or-other and the blizzard
of 20-something and I'm worried a former Arizona
girl might not survive in sub-zero temps.

I'm also not looking forward to this inventory
thing, but Twiggy was Grams' best friend and she
works for the entertainment—not the money—so
she isn't someone I want to annoy.

She orders supplies, gets the "drawer money"
for the register from the bank each day, and seeks
out rare tomes from all over the world to add to our
collection.

Since I know absolutely nothing about running

my own bookstore and can barely navigate around the place, if Twiggy calls a meeting, I attend.

The large, intricately carved wooden door is unlocked when I arrive. Twiggy must've let herself in the side door. As far as I know, I possess the only key to the one-of-a-kind front door, but she and my dad have keys to the side entrance. I pull the chain out from under my shirt and smile as the sunlight bounces off my special key's well-worn brass surface. A weighty triangle barrel with teeth on all sides.

For a moment, I step back and study the door. A centaur chasing a maiden through delicate woodland. A faun playing a flute for a family of rabbits dancing around his cloven feet. The shadow of a winged horse passing in front of the moon. A wildcat stalking a small boy.

I kneel to get a better look at the cat. It has tufted ears and a short tail like Pyewacket. Pressing my face closer, I swear the feline has the same scratches above its left eye, but that would be too—

The heavy door swings open and knocks me to my ample behind. "Geez Louise!" I press a hand to my throbbing forehead.

Twiggy's cackle fills the street.

This would be the "entertainment" I mentioned earlier. My clumsiness provides her endless amusement.

"Just wearing the clothes ain't gonna make you more coordinated." Twiggy gestures to my yoga attire.

"I was looking at the door. That cat— Oh, never mind." I stand, brush the dust off my rear, and march inside.

"You gonna wear that getup for inventory?" Twiggy hooks a thumb through the belt loop of her dungarees, shakes her helmet of grey hair, and chuckles.

The breeze is all but gone, and I feel sweat in places I'd rather not mention, but I won't let her win. "Yep. I'm wearing it all day."

"Suit yourself, doll." She stomps past me with her usual bull-in-china-shop grace and retrieves a clipboard.

I reach for it.

She swishes it back. "No siree. You climb. I write."

"Fine. Where do we start?"

She sizes me up and shakes her head. "Well, I don't want to send you up a ladder right outta the gate." She walks toward an area beneath the Rare Books Loft.

I follow.

"We'll start you off in children's literature." She points to a long, low bookcase behind a row of rainbow-colored benches festooned with stuffed animals.

Refusing to acknowledge the insult to my dexterity, I plop down on the floor and slide out the first book on the shelf. "What do you need to know?"

"How much room is left?"

Bewilderment scrunches my face. "What? Don't you need the title or the author or a code?"

"Nah. The computer tracks all of that when I scan 'em in and out. I need to know how much room is left on that shelf, so when I go to the estate sale on Thursday, I can buy accordingly."

With extreme precision, I push the book back onto the shelf. I stand, straighten my tank top, and take a deep breath. "I'm sure you find this 'hazing the new kid' shtick amusing, but I have a murder to solve. So, if you're done pulling my leg, I'll be going."

Her face pales and her skin prickles as Grams races through Twiggy and floats directly in front of my face.

"What happened? Who died?"

Before I can answer, Twiggy whispers, "Is she here?"

"Yes," I reply and gesture to Grams' general location. "As for the murder, I'll tell you both together. This morning when I took Pye for a walk, he discovered a body on the lakeshore."

Twiggy and the ghost ask in unison, "Who?"

"Erick slipped in the back of the diner and broke the news to Odell while Dad and I were eating breakfast. It was Walter Johnson, and they think it's probably suicide."

"Not in a million years," cries Grams.

"Odell asked me to look into it."

Twiggy remains uncharacteristically silent.

Grams covers her mouth with a ring-ensconced hand. "Oh, Twiggy, I'm so sorry."

I look back and forth from the ghost to her former best friend.

"Tell her, Mitzy. She can't hear me." Grams urges me to pass along the condolences.

"Grams says she's sorry to hear about Walt." A moment of clarity hits me. "Did you know Walt?"

Twiggy remains still as a statue.

Grams swirls closer to her old friend, but looks back at me. "Rumor was that they were engaged back when I was off partying with my second husband, Max Linder. Walt had a run in with the law and he headed up to Canada—"

"He didn't come back?" I ask.

Twiggy's eyes attempt to focus on me.

Grams shakes her ghostly head. "Nope. Poor Twiggy. You know, after Max was killed in the accident, I came back injured and alone. She was my only friend. She's the one who convinced me to attend AA meetings—saved my life." Grams' eyes sparkle wistfully. "Prolonged it, at the very least."

I wave my hands to get her attention and ask the question another way. "What about Walt?"

"He got a girl pregnant up in Canada. He did the right thing by her, but he and Twiggy never spoke again."

As I stare at Twiggy's no-nonsense exterior, there's a split second where the wounded woman underneath the armor is exposed.

"Give her a hug or something, Mitzy." Grams swirls around Twiggy and manages to do nothing more than give the traumatized woman a severe case of the chills.

I step closer and give Twiggy's back a clumsy pat.

She flinches and looks at the floor. "I'll handle inventory. You get over to the diner and talk to Odell." She chokes out a ragged exhale and stomps off to the back room.

I look to Grams. "Are you sure she'll be all right? Maybe I should stay?"

Grams waves me off. "Twiggy's a tough old broad. She's been making her own way for decades. The best thing is to let her be. No sense digging up hurts that she's buried so carefully."

I shrug. So much for sharing the burden.

Grams raises a finger to respond.

I point to my lips and shake my head, but add, "I get it. Let sleeping dogs lie."

At the word "dogs" a low menacing growl emanates from Pye. He peeks down from his perch atop the half-wall separating the children's section from the rest of the bookshop. One golden eye shames me for uttering such blasphemy.

"You better get over to the diner, honey."

"Copy that." I walk toward the front door but pause when I recall my supper plans with my dad. "And you better get started on an outfit for tonight." I smile as Grams eagerly floats my way.

"What's the occasion?" She's terrible at concealing her glee.

"Dad said he wants to take me to Chez Osprey before they close for the season."

The anticipation slips from her face and is quickly replaced with longing. "I thought I squeezed every last drop from life, but I'd give up all my designer gowns for one more trip out to that island."

Desperate to lighten the mood, I chime in with, "Ahem, those are my gowns now, Missy. And I'll thank you to keep them safely in their closet heaven!"

She snaps out of her mood and chuckles. "Oh Mitzy, you're such a card!"

CHAPTER 5

THE WEATHER HAS TAKEN a sudden turn for the worse, and I break into a jog as a foreboding wind knifes across the lake and into my skin.

I fight the whistling fury of the gusts to pry open the door.

All eyes turn as I blow into the diner.

I rake my fingers through my wild, white-blonde locks and rush to a booth.

Odell catches my eye through the orders-up window and the hot oil sizzles as he drops down a basket of fries.

The booth behind me empties and I glance around. A couple of tourons (my clever compound word for tourist-morons) taking selfies or foodies or whatever in the corner, and three locals bellied up to the counter are all that remain.

Odell brings out a plate of golden crisp beauties and slides onto the bench seat opposite. "You want some?"

I stare longingly at the plate of perfectly cooked french fries. "I'm still digesting that delicious breakfast."

Half of a grin tugs at the corner of his mouth. "I can eat and talk."

Despite my verbal protest my hand seems to have a mind of its own as it reaches for a golden beauty.

He doesn't touch the fries, but instead straightens the little white tubs of fruit preserves in their plastic display case as he talks. "My dad died in a hunting accident when we were kids. My mom did the best she could, but Walt was always a handful. When the cancer took her fifteen years ago . . . Well, Walt took it real hard."

Why did that number sound so familiar? Fifteen? I look at the tattered, unused cigarette poking out of Odell's shirt pocket behind his apron strap. Oh right, he quit smoking fifteen years ago. Coincidence? I think not.

"I did my best to keep tabs on him, but he's a grown man. What could I do?"

It feels like a rhetorical question, so I refrain from answering and steal another fry.

Odell takes all the packets of jam out of the

little holder and sorts them by flavor. "He ran a pretty decent bed and breakfast out on Osprey Island and then he expanded into boat tours—the chartered fishing trips I mentioned. I thought he was doin' all right."

I nod to indicate I'm following the timeline.

All the strawberry packets go in one stack. "Then we had that dry summer. The fishing was poor and the tourist traffic dwindled, and of course, winter came early and stayed late. About six or seven months ago, a big fire destroyed his lodge out on Osprey . . ." Odell's voice fades out and he looks out the front window.

I swallow as quietly as possible and softly ask, "Did he have insurance?"

His fist comes down hard on the table, sending the tower of orange marmalades skittering.

I slide the jellies back toward his side of the table, nod encouragingly, and slip a fry into my mouth despite the stares from other patrons.

"No insurance. What's worse is that he used the inn as collateral for the whole boating business. What a mess." Odell takes a precision trimmed thumbnail to an imaginary stain on the squeaky-clean table for a moment before he resumes stacking the packets.

"Did he have to sell the boats?"

He fixes me with his intelligent coffee-brown

eyes and shakes his head. "That right there—" he gestures to me "—that's the kind of thinking that would've saved Walt's life."

I take that to mean Walt did not sell the boats and I wait for further information.

"He came to me for money." Odell swings his arm wide to include the whole diner. "It might look fancy, but most months this place is farther in the red than I'd like."

I make a mental note to ask Grams how I can use my newfound wealth to help Odell without insulting him.

"Once I turned him down he worked his way down the food chain." He rubs a hand across his lined face and exhales. "I can only imagine the kind of 'help' he uncovered." Odell presses both palms against the worn edge of the table and leans back.

I wipe my mouth with a thin paper napkin and wait an extra beat. This is the point in the movie when there's always one last sliver of crucial information. No such tidbit drops, so I ask the obvious question. "You think he took money from a loan shark?" I have no idea if that's a real-world term, but I've heard it uttered by many an actor.

"Some kind of predatory lending, no doubt." He shakes his head and looks down, no longer interested in fruited-jam segregation.

"But why would they kill him? Seems like it'd

be harder to collect the vig." I don't even have time to pat myself on the back for my stellar *Get Shorty* reference before Odell knocks me down a peg.

"Who are you? Don Corleone?" He slides out of the booth. "Look, I don't want you puttin' yourself in any danger. Just see if Silas can get a copy of the medical examiner's report and I'll take it from there."

"You bet. If the ME says murder, then I'll have a little chat with Erick." I smile too eagerly.

In spite of his ill humor, Odell's mouth turns up on one side. "I'm sure you meant to say, Sheriff Harper. And I'll be the one having that chat, Mitzy."

"Of course," I lie. It's only a little white lie though. What's a tiny fib between friends?

Odell shakes his head and returns to the heat of the kitchen.

I bus my own table and slide my plate into the dish bin behind the counter. "See ya tomorrow," I call as I exit Myrtle's Diner. I best take this opportunity to walk over to the Piggly Wiggly and get a box of Fruity Puffs and a pack of toilet paper before Grams entangles me in the lengthy process of "dressing for dinner." Except they call it supper around here—supper and pop. I grin as I walk.

Straight down Main Street to 4th. The ancient blue-and-yellow sign bears a mere hint of its original vivid coloring. I enter to the now familiar "bing-bong" and the solitary cashier turns and gives me the "locals" nod. My first few visits were met with a rapid and shockingly perky "Welcome to the Pin Cherry Piggly Wiggly. What can I help you find?" Now that she's established my resident status, I receive the far less off-putting nod. We're both relieved.

I grab a four-pack of toilet tissue and make my way to the cereal aisle. Unfortunately my simple journey is interrupted when I reach the endcap and come face-to-dangerously-straight-part with an unwelcome greeting.

"Figures you'd be the one to find his body," snipes the short and stout Deputy Paulsen.

I chew the inside of my cheek while I search for an appropriate response.

Her pudgy little hand caresses the grip of her firearm with an unnerving sense of anticipation.

I can't seem to find a reason to stifle the response that is creeping toward the tip of my tongue.

She juts her chin up at me like a schoolyard bully.

And out it tumbles. "Maybe if I keep doing your job, Erick will make me an honorary deputy." I smile tightly to conceal my utter glee.

Rage seethes in her dark eyes and her knuckles whiten as she clenches her pistol grip. She sputters and spits before she manages to snarl out her response. "Sheriff Harper knows what you're up to, punk."

Every "p" and "t" in her retort spritzes me with a mist of spittle. I pointedly wipe the spray from my face. "Enjoy your shopping, Pauly." I slip past her and allow myself a silent giggle as I strut toward the breakfast foods.

She sputters something incoherent in my wake.

As soon as I turn the corner and get out of her line of sight, I break into a run and snag a box of Fruity Puffs as I race past. Olympic relay teams would be hard pressed to master such a smooth transaction. My only goal is to make it to the register and exit the store before Deputy Paulsen can think of an actual comeback.

I am one stride from the end of the aisle and I shift my weight to take the corner at maximum speed.

How could I have known there would be an "Early Thanksgiving" display of canned pumpkin—?

I hit the tower of canned goods at top speed.

Tumbling horribly as cans sail across the grocery store like confetti from a cannon.

I manage to control my slide and protect my face. As I push up to all fours, a familiar voice delivers the *coup de grâce*.

"Ya dropped something, *deputy*." Paulsen's derisive laughter echoes off the metal ceiling and bounces up from the worn linoleum.

A pack of toilet paper and a box of Fruity Puffs hit the floor near my head.

I do not look up.

The laughter continues until the scrape of a door silences the mockery.

I collect my shopping and limp to the register.

"Clean up at the pumpkin castle," crackles over the loud speaker. The clerk looks at me as though I set out to intentionally storm her vegetable ramparts. She clacks the handset back on the hook and chomps her gum.

I set my two items on the belt.

She stares at me and chomps several more times.

I slide the items closer.

She doesn't move a finger. "That'll be thirty bucks."

I open my mouth to protest, but honestly that "fine" seems fair. I fish the money from my pocket and set it on the belt.

She does not offer a bag.

I take my shopping, dispense the customary nod, and hobble out.

CHAPTER 6

MY RETURN JOURNEY down Main Street is less a
victory lap and more a walk of shame. My knee
throbs from the embarrassing incident at the Piggly
Wiggly and the frigid air bites into my skin, adding
insult to injury.

To distract myself from the discomfort, I run
through what little I know about the body I un-
luckily discovered.

Walt Johnson's death is most likely related to
his money troubles. But in a town like Pin Cherry
Harbor, I can't picture a loan shark capable of murder. I'm going to have to extend my search radius.

If Walt were as desperate as Odell says, then he
would've cast his net far and wide to get himself out
of a tight spot. I could see if my Ghost-ma knows

anything about a possible seedy side of Pin Cherry or the surrounding communities.

But for now, I'll focus all my energy on icing and elevating my swelling knee, and eventually getting ready for dinner with my dad.

That's something I never dreamed I'd hear myself say. Dinner with my dad!

After my mom died, I used to create all kinds of fantasies that would involve me tracking down my dad or my dad finding me . . . but the common thread was always the happily-ever-after for a super unhappy child.

My actual meeting with him turned out very different from any fantasy scenario, but I couldn't be happier to have him in my life.

The cold wind sends me into a spasm of uncontrollable shivers. I shuffle-limp as fast as I can and pull open the massive carved door leading into my bookshop. Grams is waiting for me.

Despite my physical pain, I at least have my wits about me enough to look around for customers before I start babbling to my resident ghost. "I had a little accident at the grocery store."

"Oh, dear, did someone attack you?"

"No, nothing that exciting. I was trying to avoid Deputy Paulsen and instead took out a massive display of canned pumpkin!"

Ghostly laughter fills the bookshop.

"It's not funny."

"Let's see what we can do about that knee. Grab some ice from the back room and toss it in a plastic bag. You should elevate it for at least twenty minutes, but then we'll have to start evaluating your fashion options for supper!"

After collecting the ice as instructed and shelving the Fruity Puffs, I stumble toward the circular staircase and slowly pull myself up to the Rare Books Loft. I squeeze my four-pack of toilet paper under one arm and place the bag of ice in that hand, while I pull the secret candle handle with the other. The bookcase slides open with satisfying mystery and I limp into my apartment.

Grams is already in the apartment, "Sit down. Sit down. Put your leg up. I'll keep working on options." Her aura seems to glow as she swirls around and vanishes through the wall, into the closet.

I fluff the pillows on the four-poster bed and place two behind my head and two under my leg. After I manage to balance the bag of ice on my throbbing knee, I sink back into the cloud of comfort. A heaviness settles onto my eyelids and I am all too aware of last night's lack of sleep.

The happy sound of Grams arguing with herself over colors and fabrics transports me to dreamland. My vivid naptime fantasies include a world where Sheriff Harper returns my affections and

Walt is miraculously resuscitated so he and Odell can repair their relationship before it's too late—

"...too late! Mitzy, you have to wake up. You're sleeping too late!" The keyed-up voice of my Ghost-ma penetrates the fog of my glorious siesta.

"I'm up! I'm up!" I'm not actually up, but I shout my irritated-to-be-awakened response and rub the sleep from my eyes. The bag of ice on my knee has turned to tepid water and has a slow leak in one corner. I hoist my leg up and push the pillows out of the way so I can stumble to the bathroom and pour the rest of the "bag water" down the drain.

"Finally," she mumbles as she drifts back into the walk-in.

After I lower myself on the padded mahogany bench in the center of the closet and get my leg situated comfortably, I gesture for Grams to hit me with the details.

"Well, dear, I tried to pick something practical since you'll have to walk down the wooden dock, climb into a boat, ride across the windy lake, and climb out on the other side."

The dress she selected is lovely, curvy, and snug. I'm happy to note that there won't be any wind blowing up my skirt. She also selected a sensible yet stylish kitten-heel that flares out at the base. And if I know my grams, that flare is exactly too wide to slip between the planks on the dock. "You thought of everything."

"Like I said, dear, Chez Osprey is one of my favorite places. I made countless trips during my healthy years in Pin Cherry. I hope you and Jacob have a memorable evening."

"Thanks Grams." My stomach growls rudely. "I think I'm going to text Dad and see if we can do an early dinner, or supper. All this knee cracking nonsense made me miss lunch." I fire off a quick text and Jacob replies that he is more than happy to meet up sooner. He even offers to come and rescue me from Grams, but he puts "Grams" in brackets. Time to get ready. I chuckle as I set down my phone and return my focus to my primary mission. "Anything I should know about the island?"

"Well, I haven't been for some time. That is, before I died. Obviously, I haven't been since."

"Obviously." I nod for her to continue.

"But in its heyday, Osprey Island was a magnificent oasis. A beautiful inn, five-star restaurant, and gorgeous hiking trails through pine-and-birch-covered hills." Grams shakes her head. "Near the end, I heard rumors that things had shifted a bit. There were a couple of new establishments on the island and some of them were run by less than reputable owners."

"Did you ever go to Walt's place?"

Grams takes a minute before she answers. Her gaze is serious. "Odell warned me to stay away from Walt's place. He was worried his brother would try to shake me down for cash."

"Did he?"

"What do you mean, dear?" The innocence in her ethereal eyes makes her look twenty-five. Which is about ten years younger than her chosen "ghost age" of thirty-five.

"I don't know everything about you, Grams, but I've learned enough to know that you seldom do as you're told. So, when you went to Walt's place, did he ask for money?"

Grams clutches one of her many strands of pearls and giggles. "Oh Mitzy, you know me better than you think. Walt's place was no Chez Osprey, but it was a nice place for families and hunters. His Canadian wife had left him to raise his daughter on his own and the sight of the little girl's poorly fitting clothes broke my heart. I told him I couldn't give him a loan, but I offered to pay for clothes for little Diane, and the gas to get her across the lake to school on a regular basis."

"Did you ever check and see if he actually used the money for the daughter?"

Guilt flickers across her face. "I was busy with the bookshop."

We wordlessly agree to shelve that conversation

and I get ready for my outing with Jacob in relative silence.

However, when the intercom buzzes, I feel completely unprepared despite the fact that I picked the earlier time. I mean, I'm technically ready, but I feel like a girl getting ready for her first father-daughter dance. I press the mother-of-pearl inlaid button and say, "Come on up." Anxiety pushes my voice an octave higher, but I force myself to plunk down on the overstuffed settee and wait patiently.

The hidden bookcase door slides open and Jacob Duncan makes his entrance.

Grams gasps. "Oh, my handsome boy."

"Dad, you look amazing. Where did you get a suit?"

"My wardrobe does consist of more than prison coveralls, Mitzy."

At first I feel terrible for my thoughtless comment, but then I catch the sparkle of mischief in my dad's eyes. "You got me," I concede.

He chuckles. "Good thing we saved you a drive out to the estate. I remember how long it used to take my mother to get ready—"

Jacob's skin prickles as Grams swirls around him in protest.

"I don't think she appreciated that remark." I point to his goosebumps.

"Why don't you get them?" he asks.

"I'm no paranormal expert, but I've always been able to see her and communicate with her . . . Maybe it's different for me."

His eyes search the air and come up empty. "Well, wherever you are Mom, thanks for bringin' Mitzy into my life."

Ghostly tears spring to her eyes and she gushes, "Oh my! Tell him how much I love him, Mitzy."

I relay the message and smile warmly at my dad.

He takes an awkward breath and blinks back his emotion. "What are we waiting for? Let's get down to the docks and head out on the lake."

I wink at my Ghost-ma. "Bye, Grams."

"Have fun, dear." Her eyes hold equal parts joy and sadness.

When we reach the slip where Dad parked the Duncan yacht, the docks and Final Destination are bustling with workers and patrons, but I'm happy to report no sign of Gary. The wind picks up and the waves on the lake turn rough and choppy. Before I have a chance to shiver, my father slips off his suit coat and drapes it over my shoulders. "Thanks, Dad."

"Happy to do it sweetheart."

The warmth created as my heart swells with love is more powerful than any insulating effect of the woolen suit coat. He helps me board the yacht and we weigh anchor for Osprey Island.

The lake is frightening and powerful this close-up, not quite the "fun" I had anticipated. The waves are massive and my stomach churns.

"I suppose I should've told you to take some motion-sickness pills," says Jacob.

"You'd think it would've been something that over-prepared Grams might have mentioned."

"Try to focus your eyes straight ahead and imagine you're riding a horse." My dad looks at me and shrugs. "Whenever Cal took me out on the lake, he used that analogy to help calm my stomach."

"So you're telling me motion sickness is hereditary?"

"Sorry." He grins sheepishly.

I attempt to implement my father's suggestion. However, I haven't ridden a horse since fourth-grade summer camp. The violent chopping of the waves and the wholly unsteady feeling under my feet is nothing like my faint memories of equine adventures.

By the time we reach the docks at the foot of the impressive Chez Osprey, my stomach is in full protest.

"You are definitely a shade of green," says Jacob.

I nod and clamp my lips together. I refuse to throw up in front of all the patrons of a fancy restaurant, or worse, stain my grandmother's cobalt-blue vintage couture.

Jacob disembarks first and offers me a hand. He steadies me as we walk down the long wooden dock and offers me a seat on an ornate carved bench tucked under a massive pine tree. "Let's just sit here a minute on *terra firma* and let your stomach settle. What do you say?"

"That sounds fantastic." I gaze over the frightful grey waters where several smaller boats in a tight group race across the angry waves. "They don't seem to be suffering any setbacks from the weather."

"I don't imagine weather or anything else gets in the way of guys like that."

I pull my gaze from the lake and stare at my father's clenched jaw. "What do you mean?"

He shakes his head.

"Seriously, Dad. What are you saying?"

A hardness sets into the planes of his face and he speaks without emotion. "That larger boat in the center is carrying contraband. The two boats on either side carry gunners and cell-jamming equipment. Redundancy is key. The boat in the rear watches the radar. They have to remain in a tight formation to appear as a single vessel. If anything comes within their safety ring, they go silent and shoot to kill." He exhales and looks at the crushed granite beneath the bench.

My chest tightens and I'm desperate to diffuse the horrible prison memories that must be rolling through my dad's head. I choose one of my classics: gallows humor. "So you think the Canadian syrup lords are bringing in some hot maple?"

He turns and his angry scowl melts into shock and finally amusement. "Somethin' like that." He chuckles again and pats my knee. "We better get in there before they give our table away."

I glance around at the "no one" queuing up and gingerly rise to a shaky, but standing, position. "Let's do this."

Jacob offers me his elbow and we walk up the steps toward an impressive split-rock entrance punctuated by thick pine double doors.

Before he can reach the handle, the door opens and a young man dressed like Daniel Boone, complete with raccoon-tail cap, waves us inside. "Welcome to Chez Osprey. The finest vittles in the north."

"Thank you," I say.

"The Maiden of the Lake will seat you."

The Native American headdress with a single— I'm assuming, osprey—feather and the buckskin shift must be the most politically incorrect restaurant uniform in the history of ever, but at least the girl looks to be of native descent. I'm actually not sure if that makes it better or worse.

"Welcome to Chez Osprey and Fish-Hawk, the sacred island of the Anishinaabe. I hope you will enjoy the food of my people." She picks up two menus and walks toward the dining room. Her warm-brown moccasins make a light swish across the polished wooden floor.

Jacob and I follow. The click-clack of my heels seems disrespectful. A few early-bird diners look up, but most ignore my entrance.

"Water from the island's spring will be served. Can I get you a birch beer or the wine list?"

I shrug and nod toward my father.

"Bring us two birch beers and some bannock."

She smiles and slips away.

A strange silence hangs in the air and I catch Jacob staring out the window with a pained expression tightening his jaw.

"So you used to come out here with Cal and Isadora, I mean, Grams?"

His eyes are slow to focus on my face and his mouth hangs open for a moment before he responds. "The last time was when they celebrated my high school graduation." He takes his napkin and lays it in his lap.

A server dressed in black trousers and a long-sleeved black button-down fills our water glasses and departs.

Jacob looks at my eyes, but I don't feel as though he sees me.

"I felt invincible that day. Cal made a grand gesture and promised to buy me any car I wanted if I kept my GPA at 3.5 or above for my entire freshmen year at college. Isadora shed a few tears and gave a water-glass toast that got the attention of the entire restaurant. The owner came out and offered Cal an expensive bottle of champagne from his private reserve."

"But Grams is an—"

"Oh, I know the drill, Mitzy. Isadora went to meetings every week and Cal would tag along at least once a month. Reminders were given, sobriety chips were displayed . . . The owner begged our pardon."

"Did it embarrass you that Grams was an alcoholic?"

"Who knows what motivates a spoiled rich kid, eh? As soon as the big showy supper ended, my buddy Darrin picked me up and we drank a case of Hamm's down at the cove and nearly drowned taking a drunk skinny dip."

I wasn't sure which part of this rattlesnake to grab. "Are you an alcoholic?"

"Me?" Jacob's eye's narrowed and he shook his

head slowly. "Nope. I got zero excuses for my behavior."

I felt bad for Grams and I snapped, "Alcoholism isn't an excuse. It's a disease."

He finally surfaced from his dive into memory pond and nodded his agreement. "I get that now, but as a kid it was harder to be objective."

The birch beers and bannock arrive. The distraction sends me down a self-reflective spiral.

That tunnel vision of childhood was all too familiar. As a young orphan, I had convinced myself that Jacob had abandoned my mom and me. While in reality, she could've called him anytime but chose not to drag her one-night-stand into unplanned fatherhood. Dreams of a father desperately searching for me had kept an eleven-year-old girl from giving up on life. Truth is a double-edged sword. Now that I know the rest of the story, it's up to me to build a relationship with my dad.

I work a dense yet flavorful bite of bannock around and wash it down with a tentative sip of clear birch beer. The crisp earthy flavor with its whisper of mint is a pleasant surprise. I set my glass on the table and catch my dad watching me wistfully. "Did you know Walt Johnson?" I ask.

Jacob grins. "You're a big fan of left field, aren't you?"

"I wanted to change the subject and that body

just loomed up in my mind. I've been told that I don't have a social filter."

"What's that supposed to mean?"

"Back in Sedona my friends frequently referred to me as Loose Lips, or sometimes just Cake Hole, because I also enjoy dessert. Not relevant, but I was always the one in the group that would ask the outrageous questions or proposition guys way out of my—"

Jacob holds up a hand for me to stop. "I'm not sure I want to hear this unsavory story about my baby girl." He chuckles, shakes his head, and takes a long drink of his water.

I mentally slap myself on the forehead. What a stupid thing to say to my dad. My cheeks are flushed and I gulp some water in hopes of cooling my skin.

He graciously changes the subject. "I don't remember much about Walt. I knew he was Odell's brother and I probably heard Isadora mention him once or twice, but we never went to the lodge, or even to that side of the island. I don't think Cal liked her to have anything to do with the Johnson men."

"Makes sense." However, I had learned a slightly different version of history. "Would it surprise you to learn that Grams did visit Walt's place and even gave him money for his daughter's clothes and education?"

Jacob raises one eyebrow. "It shouldn't. That woman never listened to anyone." He smiles appreciatively. "You're very much like her."

I furrow my brow. "Thanks. I think."

CHAPTER 7

THE REMAINDER OF DINNER is all business—the eating business. The Maiden of the Lake and her cohorts do not disappoint. Locally harvested onion and mushroom soup, wild rice, venison loin stuffed with blueberry and watercress, and a sumptuous dessert of acorn flour crepes with braised crab apples in maple syrup.

Despite my slightly distended abdomen, I'm not quite satisfied. "Dad?"

Jacob takes a sip of his roasted chicory "coffee" and grins. "I'm beginning to recognize that tone, and it sounds like I'm about to be wrapped around your little finger." He sighs and leans back in his plush leather chair.

"Do we have time to visit Walt's place on the island?"

He nods, wipes his mouth, and places his napkin on the table. "Let me see if the Duncan name can get me a quad or a couple horses. Not that you're dressed for either, but if you want to see the charred ruins of a dead man's dream—who am I to say no?"

"Thanks, Dad." I smile gratefully, but the idea of bouncing along on a four-wheel bucket of bolts or a four-legged bag of bones does not delight.

Jacob returns with a spring in his step. "Turns out Cal and Nimkii were lifelong hunting buddies. He was looking for a way to pay his respects, so supper is on the house and he'll have two mustangs saddled and waiting out front in about fifteen minutes." He places a small pottery mug in front of me. "He also gave me this snakeroot tea for you, to help prevent motion sickness on the trip back. If you drink it now, he said it should kick in by the time we get back on the boat."

"Snakeroot?" Wrinkling up my nose, I take a tentative sip. The peppery-ginger flavor is pleasing, so I down the whole cup, before standing and tugging my fitted dress down. "Maybe this was a bad idea . . ."

"You can ride side saddle," offers Jacob. "Nimkii said it's a short, easy ride. We'll be back before dark."

Dark. I hadn't even considered the perils of

being in the wild northern woods in kitten heels after sunset! The Arizona desert has scorpions, rattlesnakes, tarantulas, and javelina, but the thought of coming across a moose or a bear causes an involuntary shiver.

"Are you cold?" Jacob leans toward me with concern.

I shake my head, look down at the floor, and mumble, "Bears?"

He laughs a little too long and puts a reassuring hand on my shoulder. "Too far south for the polar variety and I don't know many black bears that can swim this far out."

I huff my annoyance and walk toward the entrance.

"Daniel Boone" appears from a side hall and scurries to open the front door.

I nod and display a half-smile.

Jacob stops and gives the guy a big handshake. "My daughter and I are going for a quick ride over to the old Walleye Lodge and Tavern. If we're not back by sunset, you get your rifle and come find us." He slips a wad of bills into the young man's hand and pats him on the shoulder.

The boy looks down at the veritable fortune in his fist and enthuses, "Yes, sir. I don't have a rifle, sir, but I'll bring Mr. Nimkii. He's a deadeye shot."

"Thanks." Jacob nods and follows me out the door.

I lean in and whisper toward his ear, "Should I be worried?"

"Not at all. I never had to work as a kid. Cal and Isadora spoiled me. I was just looking for an excuse to pass along my good fortune since I inherited my father's estate."

I smile with pride. "That was really nice, Dad."

"I'm full of philanthropic generosity. I have Cal's, I should say, my lawyer working on a legal defense fund for wrongly accused prisoners and a job placement resource, too. I know I joke about how tough things were after I got out—but it's no joke. Not many businesses wanna hire a felon."

I nod, but can't begin to understand the true price of my father's wayward choices.

The clickety-clacking of horseshoes on the wide flagstone path heralds the arrival of a youthful stable hand and our two mounts. A large red horse with a flowing mane and a spirited gate, and a smaller, tan, more subdued equine with short dark spikes of hair down its neck follow the kid.

"I'll take the tan one," I call.

My father chuckles. "When discussing horse-flesh that color is called roan, and the large mare is chestnut."

I scowl. "Fine. I'll ride the *roan* mare."

"Starlight is a male, a gelding," the boy announces. "He's real gentle."

I fume silently. So I'm not a horse expert, but I'm not an idiot. I'd like to see one of these two make a half-caff, skinny, caramel macchiato without any help.

Jacob walks over and pats the chestnut mare on the head. "What's her name?"

"That's Cranberry," the helpful lad answers.

My dad boosts me up and I take a shaky perch on Starlight while he whips his leg up and over Cranberry's back like Wyatt Earp.

The stable hand gives our horses a little swat on the rear ends and Jacob and I begin our adventure. It only takes me a couple of minutes to realize that riding sidesaddle is my only option in this tight-fitting ensemble. I hike up my dress and hook my knee over the saddle horn. From what little I recall, this is acceptable horsemanship. Most of my bare, left thigh is exposed, but at this point I don't really care about decorum, I just want to keep from falling on my backside in the middle of the woods.

"How you doing back there, Mitzy?"

I take a moment before I answer. "I'm hanging in there."

Jacob chuckles. "You want to pick up the pace?"

"That's a hard pass." I exhale loudly to indicate my utter lack of amusement.

The sun filtering through the dense pine-and-birch forest is mesmerizing. I lose track of time and slip into a daze. I completely understand why Grams loves this place. There is only the wind fluttering through the leaves and the soft thud of horses' hooves on the well-worn trail.

"Did you hear anything from Silas regarding the medical examiner's report?" asks Jacob.

I nearly lose my tenuous hold and slide right off my saddle from the shock of the voice piercing my trance. Once I regain my balance and let my heart beat return to a normal rate, I reply, "Nothing yet. But don't you think it's strange there wasn't any gossip in town about an explosion or some kind of fire?"

"I do."

The tone in my father's voice indicates so much more than agreement. "So you think Odell is right? You think someone killed Walt?"

"Not sure. It's not like Walt and I were close. And as you know, I only recently got back to town myself."

I didn't want to intrude on the beauty of this island forest with a heart-to-heart discussion about my dad's time in prison. I return the discussion to Walt. "Maybe we'll find something in the ruins that will help us figure out what happened to him."

Jacob responds by pulling back on his reins and

uttering a commanding "whoa." He dismounts with grace and skill.

I attempt to follow suit, but experience less success with Starlight. He tosses his head frantically and sidesteps. I slip back and forth on the saddle and have to drop the reins to grab hold with both hands and prevent a fall.

Jacob grasps my horse's bridle and whispers a few calming words. He wraps both sets of reins around a low tree branch and helps me dismount.

As we give the horses a wide berth, the remains of the Walleye Lodge and Tavern spread out before us. I am surprised to see a small travel trailer parked beside the charred carcass.

Jacob puts a hand on my arm and we both hesitate.

"Hello? Hello? Anybody home?" says Jacob.

No response.

We approach the trailer and Jacob knocks firmly, but not threateningly, on the small door.

It does not open.

Before I can mention that I might have heard a clicking sound, my father shoves me firmly away from the door and puts his body between the trailer and me.

"Hey, it's Jacob Duncan. Not a looky-loo. Not the sheriff. We were friends of Walt's. My mom,

Isadora Duncan, used to be married to Odell. We don't want any trouble."

He backs farther and farther away from the trailer, pushing me behind him as he speaks.

The door to the trailer swings open and the menacing double barrel of a shotgun appears followed by the determined face of the young woman whose finger covers the trigger.

Her coal-black eyes scan Jacob up and down. She leans left to get a glimpse of me in my hiked up dress and kitten heels, and chuckles. "So you finally got out of the big house, eh Jacob?"

My dad nods solemnly. "That's right. And this is my daughter, Mitzy." He steps to the side and I peek around his large shoulder.

"I'm Diane. Walt's kid." She lowers the gun, but she doesn't set it down. "If you're looking for my dad, he left on a fishing trip a few days ago, and I don't expect him back until day after tomorrow, eh."

I squeeze my hand around my dad's arm and suck in my breath. She doesn't know. We are going to have to figure out how—

"Diane, I hate to be the one to tell you, but he won't be coming home." Jacob's voice cracks a little when he says "home."

Her hand tightens around the barrel of the gun and it shakes a little. "What'd you mean?" She smooths her sleek black hair back from her high cheekbones and the nostrils of her proud nose flare slightly.

"The sheriff found a body washed up on Boilerplate Beach this morning. I'm sorry to say the tattoos identified him as Walt Johnson. I'm sorry for your loss, Diane."

"What are you talking about? No one called me. I think if—my dad was dead, someone would call me, you know." She breathes rapidly and her eyes glisten.

"Does anyone know you're living out here?" Jacob shrugs and adds, "I'll admit, I just got back into town, but I had no idea anyone was living out here."

Diane leans the gun up against the trailer and sinks onto the creaking metal step below the door. The whole trailer shifts toward her weight. She doesn't cry, she shakes her head and mumbles.

"Is there anything we can do for you, or get for you?" I ask, helplessly.

She doesn't look up but continues to shake her head. "I told him not to mess with those guys. Geez, I warned him."

Jacob takes two careful steps in her direction and stops when she looks up. "Which guys?"

She buries her face in her hands. "Never mind. It's done and dusted."

Her sleeves fall back and reveal a delicate vine

of ivy leaves encircling her right arm. Where have I seen that? Before I can stop it, the image of the body on Boilerplate Beach looms in my mind. The mermaid tattooed on Walt's right shoulder had a vine of ivy wrapped around its own right arm. Both father and daughter shared this image of remembrance for a woman who had abandoned them. I wonder if Ivy knows how much Walt and Diane miss her?

Emotions are swirling too close to the surface for me. "We're sorry to have bothered you, Diane. We should get back to the mainland." I tug Jacob's sleeve. "Let us know if there's anything we can do," I call out as we walk toward the horses.

Diane doesn't look up. Her hair covers her stoic face and the tendrils of ivy are lost under a curtain of black. She doesn't wave or make any attempt to stand.

Part of me wants to try to use my gift to pick up on her feelings, but I'm all too familiar with the feeling of helplessness that follows hearing this kind of news. I wish I could tell her I've been there and it gets better with time, but that would be a lie. Every day I was in foster care, every new placement, was just a painful reminder of the fact that I had no mother. No family in the whole world to take me in and care for me when I needed it most. I'm immensely grateful my grandmother left me her bookshop and her fortune, but I would've been so much more thankful if she had scooped me up and pieced me together when I was a shattered, homeless eleven-year-old.

Jacob gives a final wave to Diane's bowed head, and Cranberry leads the way back to Chez Osprey.

CHAPTER 8

THE RETURN TRIP across the lake to Pin Cherry is quiet. Quiet in that there is no conversation. Nature however, puts on quite a show. The waves surge, the wind rips across the massive lake, and the boat's twin engines strain to fight their way to shore as the sun slips into the indigo horizon. I'm grateful for Nimkii's effective tea taking on the monumental task of keeping down my supper.

Jacob flanks the dock with the practiced ease of a seasoned northshoreman. He leaps onto the thick weathered planks, rope in hand, and secures the boat.

I grin and imagine what it would've been like to grow up in Pin Cherry, enjoying fishing, swimming, and boating with my father.

"Mitzy?"

"Um, yeah?"

"Where did you go? I called your name three times." He smiles, but looks concerned.

I swallow the truth. "Just distracted with all the Diane stuff."

Jacob takes my hand and helps me transfer from tilting watercraft to wooden pier. Before he releases my hand, he mumbles, "I'm sorry about your mom. I'm sorry I wasn't there for you."

"Mmhmm. I know." I pull my hand free and cross my arms over my stomach. The mood ring on my left hand shimmers a purplish-grey—which is new. Maybe that's the color for the mood of resentment. I look down at the evenly spaced boards and focus all my attention on placing my feet to carefully avoid jamming a heel between two planks. It's not an actual possibility, but the false task prevents a deeper dive into dead-mom talk. A topic I prefer to avoid at all cost.

Jacob drives his pickup truck with determined caution and drops me under the street light in front of the Bell, Book & Candle.

I decline his offer to walk me up to the apartment.

Grams is hovering behind the thick wooden door of the bookshop—swirling anxiously.

As soon as I see her ghostly presence, I burst into tears.

She circles around me. "These darn useless ghost arms! I need to give you a proper hug."

I nod, swipe at the saltwater on my cheeks, and run up to the apartment.

Grams materializes next to me as the bookcase door slides closed. "What happened?"

I kick off the shoes and shake my head. "I need a shower. Alone." I catch the hurt in her eyes as I give her the brush off, but I keep walking toward the bathroom.

I turn the water on full blast and drop my dress in a heap on the floor.

The hot water pummels the tension in my neck and shoulders. My tears mix with the spray as I shove my face directly into the pulsing streams.

Steam fills the room. Time melts away.

This luxury of a hot and uninterrupted shower is something I've come to appreciate more than I ever dreamed possible. There is no privacy in foster care and no time for self-indulgence. I lived with good families and bad. Foster mom #3 and foster mom #9 were kind and generous women. Number three gave me a sense of place and the courage to embrace my intelligence. Number nine gave me enough love to allow me to accept my wider than average hips and my unusual bone-white hair. It was the first ounce of self-acceptance I learned. But no one ever let me talk about my mother. No one ever let me weep, rage, or sit silently and remember. My belongings got packed in trash bags and my feelings got buried—deep.

But today something cracked open. I know how Diane feels and I'm not going to let Walt's death be swept under the rug of small-town propriety.

I turn off the water, smooth back my hair, and let the rivulets trickle down my back. I reach through the steam for a towel to wrap around my torso, like every A-list actress in the movies, and walk out of the bathroom to announce my intentions.

I make it exactly one half a footstep out the door before Grams swoops down in concern.

"Mitzy, what's happened? It's so much better to talk about it. Ask for help if you need it. Don't be afraid to admit that you're powerless and that you need something, someone outside yourself, to help you work things out."

The psychobabble tainted with Alcoholics Anonymous aphorisms grated on my nerves when I first came to Pin Cherry, but now I understand that it's the way she expresses her love. She struggled through something monumental and she found a program that worked for her. I take a deep breath and accept the lifeline. "Did you know Diane was living in a tiny travel trailer on the site of the burned-out lodge?"

Her ghostly features pinch with regret. "No, I'm sorry to say. Once I got sick, I lost contact with Walt. Odell and I became quite close in my final years and I didn't want to do anything more to hurt him."

I nod. "Well, she is. She's living in a crap little trailer next to a pile of charred wood, all by herself. She didn't even know Walt was dead."

Grams drifts toward the large six-by-six windows and gazes at the brooding blue-black sky and the moonless waters for several minutes before she answers. "I'm sure she wasn't living there alone, Mitzy. I would guess that Walter was living there with her until the accident."

"It was no accident. And I intend to prove it."

Grams spins slowly and floats toward me, never breaking eye contact.

"What do you mean?"

"I saw that body. Something wasn't right. I can't put my finger on it, but I sensed something."

"Sensed? Are you embracing your gift?" Grams pushes in for a close face-to-ghost-face. "Are you saying you were reading the energy? Was it the energy of the place or of Walt's body?"

I shrug. "How would I know? This is all so new to me." I hold up my hand and spin the mood ring. "I saw plenty of energy workers in Sedona. Some were frauds but a few actually seemed authentic. I never believed in that stuff. I never gave it a second thought." I move into the closet and rummage through the drawers in search of my favorite T-shirt.

Grams floats a respectable distance outside the doorway and continues to interrogate me.

"Tell me more about what you felt. And try to remember if there was anything else. Visions. Sounds."

"There was nothing else; at least nothing I noticed. But after the initial shock and nausea, I did feel a dark energy. Is dark the right word?"

"Dark is fine, darling. You should call Silas."

Unable to find the T-shirt, I slip on a soft pair of shorty pajamas. "Yeah, he should have a copy of that medical examiner's report by now."

"I wasn't talking about any report. I meant that Silas might be able to help you understand what you're feeling."

"I am not exactly sure what I could tell him. He won't understand."

"What do you mean?" Grams places her bejeweled hands on her hips. "Silas, of all people, will be supportive of your gifts. He was a huge help to me when I was learning to hone my ability. I only ever had visions, though. Clairvoyant is what it's called. As far as we know you're clairsentient, which means you feel things. Maybe you felt something from the body's spirit or aura."

I chew the inside of my cheek and try to wrap my head around this idea. This concept that all the airy-fairy woo-woo nonsense I was exposed to while working in various coffee shops in and around Sedona, Arizona might actually be real. I mean, the last few years brought me in contact with a steady diet of vortexes, aura cleansing, chakra alignment, palm reading, you name it. But I never for one minute believed that any of it was true. And now I'm standing here talking to my Ghost-ma about energy I sensed coming from a corpse! I'm going to need to sleep on this.

"I agree. A good night's sleep—"

I stare daggers at Grams and point meaningfully to my lips.

"I'm sorry, dear. You're right. Your lips didn't move and it's none of my business. You get some sleep. We'll talk about it more tomorrow."

I'm in no mood to touch the gun we found under the bed. The gun that is now resting on the right side of my bed like a dangerous lover. I choose to ignore it and hope it will return the favor.

Tucked between 800-thread-count Egyptian cotton sheets, I find no peace. Images of the body on the rocks, twisting vines of ivy, and Diane's heartbreaking trailer spin unceasingly in my mind. I stretch my arm to the right and feel for the coarse but reassuring fur on Pyewacket's front paw. He yawns and his whiskers tickle my arm as he moves closer. I scratch his wide skull between his lovely tufted ears and deep-throated purring shakes the bed.

CHAPTER 9

THE NEXT THING I KNOW, the crisp light of morning in almost-Canada is blasting through my windows and jolting me upright. Note to self: maybe invest in some blackout blinds.

"It's rather late, dear. You should get down to the diner and let Odell know what's going on."

I hastily change from my flimsy PJs into my standard jeans and T-shirt. This tee features a jumble of Scrabble tiles with the tagline, "I just bought this book at IKEA."

Hurrying across the loft and down the spiral staircase, I carefully step over the "No Admittance" sign chained across the bottom.

"I thought I heard you thundering down the stairs." Twiggy appears from the back room, cup of black coffee in hand.

"I've got to head down to the diner and talk to Odell. You need anything from Rex's?"

An amused smile parts Twiggy's lips. "Look at you running around town like a local. Nah, I don't need nothin'."

A quick nod and I leave through the side door. Once in the alley, I slip my grandmother's mood ring out of my pocket and push it carefully onto the ring finger of my left hand. The small oval stone stares up at me like a dead piece of coal. Today it refuses to change colors or share its shimmering secrets. The more I stare, the less it cares. I shove the ring back in my pocket and make my way through the brisk morning breeze to the best cup of coffee in town.

I push open the door to Myrtle's Diner and Odell's normally welcoming eyes are filled with questions. I slide into a booth and Tally sets down a steaming mug of coffee and a small melamine bowl of individual creamers. I nod my thanks.

"He's crankier than usual today. Looks like he hasn't slept."

The top of the creamer peels back easily and I watch the white liquid cloud the oily black surface of my java. I swirl the spoon slowly and savor my first sip.

There are three other patrons. Two regulars at the counter and someone tucked behind a newspaper at the table in the far corner. His well-shined shoes look expensive. Not from around here. I roll my eyes and chuckle. Wow! I'm turning into a bona fide local.

A crash in the kitchen pulls my attention to the orders-up window. Tally races out with a broom and Odell returns to the grill. His mouth pinched in a hard line, his movements tinged with anger.

The door scrapes open and I instinctively turn my head. Silas Willoughby nods and slides into the red-vinyl bench seat opposite mine. He lays a small folder on the table and pushes it across.

"Bright morning to you, Mitzy. I believe this missive contains much-anticipated information."

I spin the folder around and scan the contents. The ME's report does not disappoint. They're ruling Walt's death a homicide. A few unexpected tears try to escape, but I blink them back as I close the folder. Of course, this means Erick will be looking into the murder and I'll have to play nice with Deputy Paulsen, but at least there's a chance Diane will get some justice.

Odell delivers a new plate with a fresh breakfast to my table and nods toward the folder. "That it?"

"They ruled it a homicide," I say with a slight crack in my voice.

"You on the case?"

"I already was."

Silas interrupts our terse exchange with his order. "I'd like to partake of the special, if it's not too much trouble."

Odell nods and walks back toward the kitchen.

I call out quietly, "I met Diane yesterday."

His footsteps hesitate, but he seems to change his mind about something. Odell does not return to the table.

Silas harrumphs once and chews the corner of his mustache.

"What?" I ask.

"They are not close. Odell never trusted Diane's mother, Ivy. In fact, I seem to remember him inventing a clever moniker—something akin to 'Evil Ivy.' Drove a wedge between him and his brother, and therefore between him and his niece. Regardless, Ivy caused a great deal of trouble for Walter back in the day. She was a woman of ill repute."

I stare at Silas and shrug. "Is that supposed to mean something to me?"

"In your jargon, I believe she would be referred to as a lady of the night, or perhaps a gentleman's hostess?"

I nearly spit take my coffee. "In my jargon, she'd be a prostitute."

Silas is obviously offended by my base language.

"It is my understanding that she danced for payment. I am not aware of any escort services."

"So, a stripper." I take another sip of my wake-up juice.

He shakes his head and frowns. "As you will. However, she took a sizable portion of Walter's money and saddled him with a daughter, whom she clearly never desired. The poor man did his best with Diane, but if your grandmother hadn't intervened on behalf of the girl's education . . . I fear things might have been far worse."

"Diane is living in a thimble-sized trailer beside a pile of rubble. Things got worse."

"And why would this be any of your concern, Mitzy?"

"I know what it's like to lose the most important person in your life and be left with nothing." I stare into the old man's milky-blue eyes for a second before my gaze drops to my untouched breakfast.

"I acknowledge your frustration. But your situations are far from similar. Diane is a full-grown woman with a nearly achieved bachelors degree and the ability to make a new life for herself."

"Walt left her nothing but a mess. He had no insurance on anything and his boats are most likely going to be repossessed. The trailer she's living in probably isn't even paid for!"

"I fail to see the connection between Diane's

problems and your tone. However, if you feel some philanthropic urge, I am certain we can allocate funds to assist Walter's offspring in her time of supposed need."

I lean back and gaze at Silas, taking in his smooth shiny head, unperturbed expression, and rumpled tweed coat. He's right. I can afford to help Diane. I've never been in a position to help anyone before. The thought never occurred to me. I pick up my fork and dive into my lovely scrambled eggs and perfectly browned home fries.

"So where's this Ivy chick now?" I mumble through a mouthful of food.

"Manners, Mitzy." Silas carefully places a paper napkin on his lap and pulls a second one from the dispenser at the end of the table to tuck into his collar and protect his faded bowtie. "It is my understanding that Ivy returned to Canada once she had bilked young Walter of his funds."

"Nice girl." I roll my eyes. "Any chance you have a connection at Immigration? I mean, INS?"

The vinyl creaks as Silas leans back and strokes his thumb and finger down across his bushy mustache. He almost grins. "A fascinating idea. Is there something you're not telling me?"

My fork halts midway between my nearly empty plate and my full mouth. My eyes tentatively look up toward Silas. There is a strange, commanding power in his eyes, not the aged tired man who stared across the table earlier. I lower my utensil, pick up my napkin, and swipe it across my mouth. "What are you talking about?"

"I am certain you know exactly what I'm talking about, Mizithra."

He uses my proper name. My throat tightens. He senses something. Is it my posture? Can he see my aura? I have zero experience interacting with alchemists, so I'm not sure if this question is genuine or if he's testing my honesty. Grams thinks he can help me understand my gifts, but . . . I suddenly have to wonder why the immigration idea *did* pop into my head? Did I think it up or did that idea come from somewhere beyond me? Maybe I do need help. I swallow hard and lower my shaking hands to my lap.

He leans forward and his eyes seem to bore into my soul. "Go ahead. I'm listening."

"Grams, er um Isadora, wanted me to tell you. But I don't know—I'm not sure—it seems crazy."

"If your grandmother feels it is pertinent, I propose that it behooves you to share your news."

A calm sensation floods over me and I breathe a huge sigh of relief. Did Silas do something? I guess it's now or never. "She thinks I might be clairsentient. Maybe she's projecting, or it's wishful thinking. But that's what she wanted me to tell you."

Silas inhales and steeples his fingers beneath his jowls. "I suspected as much. Has she given you the ring?"

My hand involuntarily touches the lump in my left pocket.

He nods. "She has."

"That's creepy. How did you know?"

"I observed your hand move, dear. No magic involved."

"Do you think I have an actual gift, or whatever?"

"Tell me exactly how events unfolded when you placed the ring on your finger."

"Do you mean today or the first time?"

"Both. Begin with the first time."

My fingers trace the outline of the ring in my pocket as I speak. "I was messing around in her jewelry box, and for some reason I slipped that particular ring on my finger. At first the stone was totally black, so I asked what kind of ring it was. Then Grams spent all this time explaining what a mood ring is and went on and on, and to be honest I kind of zoned out. But when I looked back at the ring, it wasn't changing to any of the colors she mentioned. It looked like it was moving, like there was a storm inside the stone. If that makes any sense?"

Silas takes a slow, measured sip of his coffee and

dabs his mustache with a napkin before he answers. "Go on."

"For a minute I felt something and it almost seemed like I saw something in the swirling mist inside the stone. I'm not sure. It all happened so fast. It was probably just my imagination playing tricks on me because of everything Isadora was saying."

"And today?"

I squeeze the ring nestled in the fabric of my skinny jeans. "Today there was nothing. I slipped it on, looked down at the stone, and it stayed black."

He drags his prayer-hands down the flesh of his chin, bounces his head lightly on the tips of his fingers, and his lips quiver with the promise of words— but no sound escapes.

"What did you say?" I ask.

"What did I feel?" he replies.

His tactic of answering my question with a question is not only irritating, but also unsatisfying. I open my mouth to toss a little snark in his direction, when a phrase pops into my head. I repeat it aloud without hesitation. "You feel curious." I jerk my head back and the hairs on my arms stand on end. A chill runs through my whole body and my mouth waters in the icky way it always does right before I throw up. I want to get up and run to the bathroom but I can't move.

"And that's your first lesson." Silas briefly smiles with a satisfaction I have never seen on his face before, and then he calmly takes another sip of coffee.

Sliding out of the booth, I stare at my lawyer. My mouth opens and shuts like a fish gasping for air, before I find my voice. "I gotta go."

He nods calmly. "Good day, Mitzy."

CHAPTER 10

BACK AT THE APARTMENT, I can't stop pacing or biting my fingernails. Which is a new bad habit, because I used to pride myself on never having such a vice. The stress of the morning, combined with the strain of not understanding my gift and the pressure to find Walt's killer—it's all too much. I gnaw viciously on another innocent fingernail.

Grams flickers in and out, desperate to help me but unable to break through my anxiety attack. "Honestly, if you just sit down and take some deep breaths, I promise it will help. I've been where you are. In truth, I've been much lower, sweetheart, but I've definitely been where you are. When I started reading those old books out there and discovered how to manage my gift, everything just made more sense to me. In the beginning, the visions are what drove me to drink, but in the end, learning how to interpret them and even use them gave me some power over my life. I may be an alcoholic in recovery, but studying the psychic arts is what saved me. I would never discount the value of the program. The program worked because I worked it. But learning to be a 'wise woman' and to embrace my visions, that's what truly transformed me."

It's possible that I've been pacing for hours or days. Maybe Grams has a point?

I lower myself onto the overstuffed settee and take three deep breaths. I don't feel better, but I do feel different.

"That's it. Now take three more."

I reluctantly follow her instructions and have to admit that my heart rate is beginning to return to normal. But before I can find any real sense of calm—

Twiggy's voice blasts through the intercom and shatters my fragile peace. "Hey, Silas is down here. He says it's important."

I exhale in frustration and press the mother-of-pearl button next to the speaker to reply. "Can you send him up, please?"

A staticky click is the only response.

The bookcase door slides open and Silas shuffles in. The meek, unassuming lawyer who stands before me bears little resemblance to the wise and powerful alchemist who sat across from me in the booth at Myrtle's Diner.

"I received some information from my INS contact." He looks at me with something like pride in his eyes. "Ivy did return to Canada after Diane was born, but she didn't stay. Or at least she didn't stay put. I've come to understand that the DEA has built quite a case file on Ivy Johnson, a.k.a. Ivy Lapointe."

"Drug enforcement?" So many things are swirling through my brain I can't grab hold of anything. Ideas. Words. Images. Some of it feels like a memory and some of it feels like a dream.

Grams rushes to my side. "Ask him if Walt was involved?"

"Grams wants to know if there's any mention of Walt?"

"There was." Silas takes a seat and waits.

"Well, what did it say?" I ask. But before he can answer, I fire off several more questions. "Was Walt implicated in some kind of drug scheme? What would they even be doing? She's in Canada, right? Is there some kind of illegal maple syrup trade?"

"To address your last question first, yes there is. However, Ivy and her cohorts were into a far more lucrative operation. They were trafficking counterfeit opioids."

Grams gasps and clutches one of the many strands of pearls around her spectral neck.

"Counterfeit opioids? And I thought meth was bad," I mumble, as I recall a foster brother who peddled that nasty crap at school . . . They didn't catch him until a high school sophomore overdosed. I probably should've turned him in, but at the time I was pretty busy fighting for my own survival.

Grams rudely ignores my reverie and blurts, "What's your next move, Mitzy?"

Her question interrupts my unhappy trip down memory lane and I stare through the grandmotherly apparition while I search for something resembling a plan. "I need to get back out to the island."

Silas stands and his mouth tightens with concern. "What are you considering?"

"I need to get back out to that island and find out what these 'other' operations are that popped up on the far side of the island."

"That sounds like neither a well-thought-out nor safe plan." He clears his throat but does not continue.

"What other choice do I have?"

"Perhaps you could convince Deputy Paulsen to do your dirty work for you." Silas tilts his head.

Talk about your impossible odds! An unsavory image of me lying on the floor of the Piggly Wiggly surrounded by the detritus of a toppled canned-pumpkin tower flashes in my mind. "I'm not sure if you've noticed, but Deputy Paulsen pretty much hates me."

Grams giggles like a schoolgirl. "And when have you ever let that stop you?"

I gasp in mock horror. "Well I never!"

Silas stares at me with concern. "I assume Isadora made some comment which you failed to share?"

I nod. "You seem to be the one with all the diplomatic gifts. What would you suggest I use as incentive for Deputy Paulsen to do my work?"

"It's my understanding that high-profile cases go a long way toward boosting one's political ambitions."

I scrunch up my face as I replay the cryptic advice from Silas. Grams moves in closer to blurt out her interpretation, but I put up a finger and motion for her to give me a moment.

Silas slips a pair of tarnished wire-rim glasses from his interior coat pocket, rubs the rose-tinged lenses, and hooks the stems over his large ears. He glances about until his gaze lands firmly on Grams. "My, my, Isadora. You are as breathtaking in spirit as you were in life. Perhaps one day, I will unearth an incantation that will bestow me with the blessed ability to hear your charming voice once again." He sighs wistfully. "But until then, I am grateful for these spectacles and their gift of sight beyond."

I turn away to hide the misty emotions clouding my vision. The bond between Silas and my grandmother, as I understand it, is completely platonic. Yet there is some deeper connection that I can't comprehend. Perhaps it's the magic? Perhaps the bond between mentor and protégé? A bond that can transcend death must be deeper than any one-dimensional love.

Grams whispers, "It is, dear. It is."

My throat feels like a tiny frog is fighting against my instinct to swallow. I cough a little before I announce my plans. "I'll head down to the police station. It's time to light a fire under this investigation into Walt's murder."

Silas nods appreciatively.

Grams gives me a slow clap and a chuckle.

I roll my eyes. And to avoid involving Silas in our teasing banter, I simply think my response. *Really, Grams? The slow clap?*

She giggles until ghostly tears touch her shimmering cheeks. I shake my head and open the bookcase door. Pyewacket bounds through the door knocking me onto the settee, which in turn jostles its current occupant, Silas.

The inconvenienced man stands and straightens his rumpled coat. "You have spoiled

every ounce of decorum out of that feline, Isadora."
He harrumphs into his mustache and exits.

"Pye, what are you up to?"

The dog-sized caracal sprawled across my bed,
next to that pesky handgun, holds something down
with one paw while tugging on a piece of it with his
dangerous incisors.

I approach to take a closer look and he gives a
low guttural warning growl.

"Look here mister, I'm the one that pours the
Fruity Puffs in this house. So if you would like to
continue to receive your pampering, then you better
show me what's under that paw."

To my utter shock, the spoiled beast pulls back
his paw to reveal a small silver key dangling from a
neon-yellow foam disc.

I reach for the object and receive no further
threats. "What kind of keychain is this?"

Grams whizzes over. "Boat key. The foam disc
floats! Isn't that clever? That way if you drop your
key overboard you have time to recover it. Isn't it
ingenious? I don't know who invented it but—"

"Grams, I don't need the whole history of
floating key chains. I grew up in the desert and
don't know a whole bunch about boats, but I get it.
Keychain floats. Probably means this is the key to a
boat. The second time I say the word "boat," I *feel*

beyond a shadow of a doubt that this is the key to Walt Johnson's boat.

"Mitzy! What does it mean?"

There's no time to scold her for eavesdropping on my thoughts. "I have no idea, Grams. I'll give it some thought on my walk down to the station."

"What about the key?"

A smile slides across my face. "I'll give it to Deputy Paulsen as a show of good faith."

"My precious little cuddle muffin knew exactly what you needed." She drags her ghostly fingers across Pyewacket's back and he arches towards her as though he can actually feel her touch.

I spin the keychain around my finger and head down to the station.

Despite my many trips to the police station since my arrival in Pin Cherry Harbor, the uniformed officer manning the front desk is a new face. "Hello there, would you happen to know if Deputy Paulsen is in this afternoon?"

Without so much as a glance in my direction he mumbles, "Take a seat. I'll let her know you're here."

"Would you like to give her a name?" I ask.

He picks up a telephone, dials a three-digit extension, and announces, "There's some lady here to see you." And he drops the receiver back into the cradle with a thunk.

Moments later, the short, squat form of Deputy Paulsen rounds the corner and catches sight of me. She halts and slides her hand down to her pistol grip. "Here to cause more trouble, Moon?"

"Not on your life, ma'am. I was actually wondering if I might have a private word?"

Her eyes narrow, and she chomps on either a cud of gum or plug of tobacco. Who could be sure?

"I'll talk to you in interrogation room one. You've got five minutes."

I obediently lead the way to interrogation room one, as my familiarity with the station extends to said interrogation rooms. She follows me in, unnecessarily kicks the door shut, and continues to fondle her weapon.

I take a seat and assume a docile and cooperative posture. "I'm sure you know that Erick—"

"Sheriff Harper."

"Of course, I'm sorry. Sheriff Harper asked me to stay out of the Walt Johnson homicide, but I have an important piece of information. The kind of information that could literally make a career in a small town like Pin Cherry. I didn't want to bother him with it, seeing as how he told me to stay out of things. But I had to tell someone, and I feel like you're the second-in-command around here." The acid roiling in my stomach will certainly give me away. I'm not sure if I can last the full five minutes with this level of suck-up-itude.

"You better not be yanking my chain, Moon. What's this information?"

"Were you aware that Walt's daughter, Diane, is living out on the island?" I'm fairly certain she knows this, but giving her the opportunity to display her superior knowledge should put me right where I hope to be.

"Between the two of us, you're the new kid in town. If that's all you got, I have a job to do."

"Of course. Of course you would know that. But, maybe you didn't know that her mother is the focus of an international DEA investigation?"

You couldn't smack the shock off her face with a baseball bat.

I swallow the smug grin struggling to display itself on my face. "Her maiden name was Lapointe. It sounds like she's part of a huge opioid smuggling ring. I mean, a bust like that—that's the stuff of legend." I clench my fists under the table and swallow everything else I want to say. The look on the deputy's face is everything.

"If the DEA is running some kind of sting in our territory, then I'm sure they filed proper paperwork. Go ahead and pat yourself on the back for being a good citizen. I'll take it from here."

I smile as innocently as I'm able. "Thank you,

Deputy. I knew I came to the right person." I drop my gaze to the floor hoping to appear humble, but genuinely wanting to hide the victory dancing in my eyes.

She grabs the door handle and motions for me to get out of the interrogation room.

"Oh, I almost forgot." I hold up the almost-glowing foam disc and dangle the silver key. "My cat brought this in. He was with me when we found — Anyway, I'm sure this belonged to Walt Johnson.

Paulsen snatches the keychain from my hand and shakes her head. "You just have a knack for destroying evidence, don't you?" She whips a plastic bag from her back pocket and drops the key inside. "Probably not a single usable print . . ." She continues to grumble under her breath.

Before I say something I'll enjoy more than I'll regret, I get myself out of the station.

Not a resounding success, but I'll take it.

CHAPTER 11

THE SUN IS HIGH OVERHEAD and the welcome warmth encourages a lazy pace down the cracked sidewalk. I'm not sure what it is about the town of Pin Cherry Harbor, but it genuinely feels like home. For the first time in a long time, I feel happy, and lucky—and loved.

Unfortunately, my half-celebration is cut short as Sheriff Erick parks next to the curb on Main Street and gets out of his cruiser. I toy with the idea of walking past without giving him so much as a glance, but when he calls out my name, I have no choice but to stop.

He steps onto the sidewalk and walks toward me with one hand extended.

I naturally walk forward to see what he has for

me. However, it isn't exactly natural. Turns out the uneven sidewalk has it in for me and two steps into my "meet cute" I catch my toe on an angled edge of concrete and crash into the deliciously firm chest of the local constable. To be fair, he doesn't exactly handle things with stunning grace himself.

"Oh shoot!" He fumbles to set me upright and brushes against my bikini-top area. "Sorry. I'm so sorry, Miss Moon." Erick steps back and rubs his hand against his pant leg as though he has touched a toad rather than my fully clothed left boob.

I choose to draw attention away from my tumble by directing a spotlight on his. "I like a guy to at least take me to dinner before he tries to get to second base."

Erick's face turns as red as a pin cherry.

"I may have to change your nickname from Sheriff Too Hot to Handle to Sheriff Too Handsy." The joke falls flat and I shrug.

He's still rubbing his hand against his pant leg and I'm beginning to feel more than a little offended.

"Did you have something for me?" I prompt.

"I think you dropped this at the crime scene." His voice is tense and his manner uncomfortable. He places a business card in my hand.

I don't have the heart to tell him that I've never

taken a business card from anyone in my entire life. So, I glance down at the card and see the name of a rare-books dealer embossed on the thick paper. Curious. Who knows where this could lead? I choose to feign responsibility. "Oh, yeah, I've been looking for that. Thanks." I move left to continue on my route back to the bookstore and he slides the same direction. I zig to the other side and he zigs the same way. I stop, smile, and glue myself to the sidewalk until he moves around me. "Good day, Erick," I call as he strides toward the station.

He mumbles a response and disappears into headquarters.

I skedaddle back to the bookshop with two new pieces of information.

Once I'm safely ensconced in my apartment, I whip out my phone and search for "Lars Gershon," purveyor of rare books and antiquities.

Grams is strangely absent from the apartment and the lack of an audience is disheartening. I offer my wonderful news to Pyewacket. "You'll be happy to know that I successfully conned Deputy Paulsen into investigating Ivy Lapointe. And that's not all I accomplished."

Pyewacket rolls onto his back, stretches lazily, and yawns.

"What else did I uncover you ask? Well, I'll tell

you. The business card of one Lars Gershon was found at the crime scene. Perhaps a coincidence. Perhaps not." I can almost hear the "dun, dun, dun" of the movie soundtrack—in my mind.

A shower of white light bleeds through the wall and interrupts my report.

"Did I hear you say something about Lars? Lars Gershon?" Grams' face is whiter than usual.

"Yeah, Erick gave me this." I fan the business card. "I looked him up and he seems to have a legit business. Or at least he seems to have a legit website."

"Oh, dear. Oh, dear, dear, dear." If Grams had corporeal legs, I would say she's pacing. But in her case, it's more like swirling or spinning.

"It sounds like you might know Lars, Grams. Is that true?"

She shimmers to a halt and fixes me with a guilty stare. "I may have had some dealings with Lars. If you know what I mean."

Just a quick reminder, my Grams is a bit of a skank.

"Now now, Mitzy, I told you there's a very wide line between a skank and a woman of means who knows what she wants."

"The line's not that wide, Grams."

She shakes her head and swirls toward the plump settee. I'm sure she thinks she's sitting on it, but from where I stand the view is a strangely unsettling, see-through, hovering sensation.

"Lars was fascinating. He was well-traveled, spoke seven languages, including Latin. And he used to bring me trinkets from all over the world."

"And how do you suppose his business card showed up next to Walt's corpse?"

"Well, I have no idea. I don't think Lars even knew Walt."

"You don't think, or you don't know?"

"That doesn't make any sense, Mitzy. What I meant to say was I never introduced Lars to Walt, and Walt never mentioned meeting him to me. But I hardly know everything that goes on in this town." Grams straightens the lovely burgundy tulle of her gown and fiddles with one of the rings on her left hand.

I step closer. "Is that a gift from Lars?"

She becomes so still I fear her spirit has somehow disconnected from the apparition.

"Grams? Grams?"

She flickers for a second before rocketing toward the coffered ceiling.

"What exactly happened between you and Lars?" I ask.

"Why don't you see if you can schedule a meeting with him."

I gaze up at my floating Ghost-ma and chew the

inside of my cheek. "That sounds a lot like you're not going to answer me. Is this misdirection or transference?"

"Don't waste your time psychoanalyzing a ghost, Mitzy. Just call the number on that business card and see if you can set up a meeting with Lars."

I tap the digits into my phone and a friendly-voiced woman with a hint of a southern accent answers on the second ring.

"Gershon Antiquities, how may I help you?"

"I was hoping to speak to Lars if he's available."

There's no response, but I know I didn't drop the call because I can hear short quick breaths on the other end of the phone.

"Hello? Do we have a bad connection?"

"Oh no, it's fine. I'm sorry. I just got the news an hour ago, and I haven't had time to figure out what to tell people. I'm sorry. It's just—"

"What news?"

"Did you know Mr. Gershon?" she asks.

I decide to fabricate what I don't know. "He was a close friend of my grandmother, Isadora Duncan."

A sharp inhalation on the other end of the line precedes the response. "Oh, my condolences."

"Sorry?"

"I'm sure she'll want to come to the funeral."

I feel like I've slipped into an Abbott and Costello routine. I can't imagine why my dearly departed grandmother would want to come to her own funeral and I'm tempted to say as much to this flighty southern belle. But I choose the "more flies with honey" option. "I'm afraid I'm a bit confused. My lovely grandmother passed away a few months ago. I was simply reaching out to Lars in hopes of gaining a better understanding of her book business. You see, I've inherited the bookshop and—"

Intense sobbing on the other end of the line interrupts my unrehearsed lie.

"Miss, are you all right?"

After two ragged gasps and one unladylike nose blowing, she responds, "Mr. Gershon is deceased. I only just received the call . . . I don't have any details. I'm so sorry."

The line goes dead. I pocket my phone and look up at Isadora. "Bad news, Grams."

She floats down with a slow and deliberate flourish. "He's gone, isn't he?"

I nod.

"When I saw that business card, I had one of my little visions. Like I used to get when I was alive. I saw his face, but it was a ghost. I haven't had any visions since I died, and I wasn't sure what to do." She floats to the window and shakes her head.

"It's all right Grams. We both have a lot of things to figure out. But one thing is for sure, there's a connection between Walt and Lars. I'm sure of it."

CHAPTER 12

THEY SAY THAT the early bird gets the worm. *They* can have their worms. I prefer to roll out of bed at the crack of 10 AM.

As soon as my feet hit the floor, Grams rushes out of the closet. "Oh good, you're finally up."

Rude.

She narrows her gaze and continues, "You should see if Jacob will take you back out to the island. Maybe Diane knows something about Lars."

"And if you would've given me a moment to wake up, that was exactly what I was about to say."

She smiles with pride. "Great minds!"

I can't handle this much perkiness before my first cup of coffee. I zombie-walk into the closet, struggle into yesterday's skinny jeans, and grab a clean T-shirt. This one sports a cuddly kitten and the tagline "You look MEOW-velous!" I slide my feet into a pair of flip-flops and stop in mid turn as my hand brushes against the ring still shoved in my left pocket.

Grams hovers just outside the closet, her face a mix of anticipation and concern.

I pull the band out of my pocket and slip it onto the ring finger of my left hand.

We both hold our breath. Although, in her case it hardly seems as noteworthy a feat as it does in mine.

"Anything?" she asks.

"No. Wait—" The black cabochon shifts in hue to a yellowish-amber. "Something's happening."

Grams floats into the closet and hovers over my right shoulder.

We watch together as the curved stone seems to simultaneously grow in diameter and depth. The scene shifts to a swirling royal blue and I swear I can almost see an island taking shape amongst the waves. "Did you see it?"

"No, dear. I saw the color change a bit, but that was all. How about you?"

"It was probably my imagination." I let my hand drop to my side. The ring feels like a ten-pound weight.

"Nonsense. You have a gift. You have to believe that. What did you feel?"

I shrug. "I didn't feel anything this time. I thought I saw water and maybe an island."

Grams inhales sharply and clutches her pearls. "You *saw* something? Have you ever had visions before?"

My mind is inundated with images from my past. I basically survived foster care by creating alternate realities within my mind. What a loaded question. I'm not exactly sure how to answer her. A hand pats my back, and I nearly jump out of my skin. "Who's there? What was that?"

"What is it, dear? What happened?"

"Someone—or something—touched my back!"

Grams moves closer to me and her ethereal fingers reach toward my arm. "Did it feel like this?"

As her ghostly energy comes into contact with my skin, a surge of unfamiliar sensations race across my skin. My eyes widen to saucers. "Yes."

"Oh, hallelujah! We've made a connection, Mitzy. I can actually touch you." Otherworldly tears spring from her eyes, and for the hundredth time I wish she'd been buried with a handkerchief.

I sink to the floor of the closet and let my head fall into my hands. What is happening to me? Visions inside rings. Physical interactions with ghosts. It's all too much for me.

Grams whispers, "I know your lips didn't move, dear. But I have to say something. You're a witch."

I shake my head and put up my hands to stop her.

"You can call it a wise woman, a psychic or an empath, if that makes you feel better. I told you before and I know you didn't believe me. But you can't continue to deny your nature. I never had your gift, or maybe gifts. I had a few wonky visions, an occasional premonition, nothing extraordinary. Most of what I learned I read in books or heard about from Silas. I practiced and practiced, but it always seemed like the more energy I tried to control the sicker I got."

I look up. "Are you saying that you died from an overdose of magic?"

"I'm sure modern medicine would have chalked it up to the predictable liver failure of an alcoholic. But I stopped drinking a long time ago. Even if you count the relapses, it was fifteen years, eight months, and three days since I had my last drink. That's counting back from the day I died of course."

"Of course." Math may not be my favorite subject, but even I can solve that equation. "The day dad went to prison?"

"Indeed. I believe the hardest thing in the world would be for a mother to lose a child. But the second hardest thing is to feel so awfully responsible for letting that same child down, and knowing that he'll waste fifteen years of his life paying for a crime he never should've committed."

"You're not responsible for his actions, Grams."

"I know. I know. Grant me the wisdom to know the difference. You'd be surprised how many times you can say that in fifteen years." She shakes her head as though the memories can be erased and returns to an earlier topic. "Anyway, Silas was quite confident that my illness was a result of overloading my system with more power than I knew how to manage. I kept studying and trying new meditations and spells, hoping one of them would help me find a way to go back in time and make different choices."

"What?"

"It was foolish. If I had spent half that time and energy on acceptance, I'd still be alive today."

I get to my feet and run my hands through my haystack of white hair. "And then I'd still be an orphan."

A beautiful light fills her eyes and her smile nearly breaks my heart. "You're right! If my death is the thing that brought this family together, I'd do it again without hesitation." She swooshes toward me, wraps her glimmering arms around me, and I feel like I've slipped into a bubble of love and protection.

I swipe at the tears adorning my cheeks and chuckle. "Time for the humans to have breakfast."

"Certainly. I'll be here when you get back."

"Speaking of breakfast, where's Pyewacket?" Grams disappears, and I make my way to the Rare Books Loft. She reappears a few moments later, giddy and bursting to tell me what she's discovered.

"Out with it." I circle my hand in the "continue" gesture.

"He's stretched across the desk in the back room and Twiggy is hand feeding him Fruity Puffs!" she whispers.

A strong urge to race to the back room and taunt Twiggy swells inside. I fight the urge.

Grams nods her approval of my decision.

"I'm off to the diner. Okay? I'll get a hold of Jacob when I get back and see if he can take me out to the island today."

"I hope he has time to stop by before you leave. I'd love to see him."

"I'll see what I can do." As soon as I step out of the bookshop, I regret my decision to leave without a jacket. But in the fight between shivering and starving, my stomach almost always wins. I break into a jog and cover the short distance to Myrtle's Diner in no time. When I open the door, I am pleased to discover my father already occupying a booth.

He waves me over and I slide in across from him. The mouth-watering smell of Odell's cooking engulfs me.

Tally is en route with my coffee and Odell salutes me through the orders-up window with his metal spatula.

Smiling at my dad, I say, "I was gonna call you after breakfast."

Jacob thoughtfully chews his mouthful of pancakes and washes it down with a swig of coffee before he replies. "What can I do for my favorite daughter today?"

"Don't you mean your only daughter? If I have a half-sibling out there somewhere, I'd like to know right now. I don't think I can handle anymore family surprises."

Jacob chuckles good-naturedly. "Nope. No siblings. Your mom was the only one who let one slip through the five-hole."

I scrunch my face in horror. "Five hole? Is that appropriate to say to me?"

He struggles to swallow his coffee and stifle his laughter simultaneously. Lucky for me, swallowing wins the battle and he avoids spewing hot coffee across the table. "It's nothing like that, Mitzy. It's a hockey term. It's the zone at the bottom of the net between the goalie's skates."

A sigh of relief escapes. "I guess I didn't learn a

lot of hockey terminology in Arizona. But I could probably tell you more than you would ever want to know about dry heat or javelina."

He nods comically. "I'm sure you could. As of right now, I have no questions on those topics."

Tally slides my breakfast onto the table and I dig in. Not as well mannered as my father, I talk with my mouth full. "Can you take me out to the island today?"

He tilts his head and eyes me suspiciously. "What do you need on the island?"

"Couple of things."

"Like what?"

I don't particularly like the set of his jaw. "I have some questions for Diane."

"And . . ."

After a few more bites of my fluffy scrambled eggs and a long sip of my wake-up juice, I answer, "I was hoping we could take a little trip around the perimeter. Maybe just get a feel for the whole island."

He sets down his fork and fixes me with a patented fatherly stare. "You don't want to poke that bear, Mitzy."

"You told me there weren't any bears on the island." I attempt to school my features into a portrait of innocence.

"Don't give me that look. You and I both know

what's happening on the other side of that island, and I'm not about to sail into those unfriendly waters unarmed."

"But I thought— I mean, it's not legal for you— do you even have a gun?"

"Yeah, I'm not about to violate my parole by carrying a gun. But you seem like a girl who doesn't know when to mind her own business—"

"Dad!" I shout my protest, but the truth is, I have no right to be offended. He couldn't be more correct.

He chuckles and adds, "What I was going to say was, I know a guy. He can teach you a thing or two about firearms. I don't want you carrying a gun without knowing how to handle yourself."

"Oh." I nod cooperatively. "But can we at least go back out to Osprey—or is it Fish-Hawk Island— and talk to Diane?"

Jacob exhales and puts his hands up in surrender.

CHAPTER 13

My second ride on the Duncan estate watercraft
is less upsetting to my stomach than my first adventure. I also remember to wear a thick hoodie and
Jacob gives me something called a "slicker." I pull
both tightly around me to keep out the biting wind.
Because as luck would have it, the second we left
the dock, black rain clouds rolled in.

Jacob shouts over the roaring twin engines,
"You okay?"

I don't bother using words. I simply nod my
head.

We take the now familiar route to the small pier
in front of Chez Osprey. With crappy weather and
choppy waves, my dad doesn't waste any time getting us across the lake.

The engine slows and Jacob slides into a slip

with ease. He jumps off the boat, ties us off, and reaches down to help me ashore.

"Nice bit of drivin' there, Dad."

He chuckles. "Didn't want to risk bringing up your fancy breakfast."

"Do you think Nimkii will let us borrow the horses again?"

"Of course." We hurry up the steps and knock on the heavy wooden door of the restaurant.

Jacob thumps his fist several times. "They're only open for supper. Hopefully somebody in the kitchen will hear us knocking."

No one answers.

"Maybe we should just go out to the stables."

Jacob looks at me and grins. "That brain of yours is always cooking isn't it?"

He leads the way around the far side of the building and I run my fingers along the curved log surface. I like the feel of the smooth logs and the pattern of dark brown knots against the pale golden timbers.

As we approach the stables, Nimkii walks out with two saddled horses trailing behind. He stops and stares at me with a strange gleam in his eye. "I see the spider brought me a message of truth."

My father and I exchange a confused glance.

"Pardon me?" I say.

Nimkii hands Starlight's reins to me as he says,

"I was told of your coming. I was told you would need horses." He gives me a slight nod and his smoothly plaited salt-and-pepper braid swishes gently.

I fear my grandmother has found a way to cut her tether from the bookstore and interfere on a broader scale. "What do you mean you were told? Who told you?"

"Today, spider was the messenger. There are many messengers. But we do not always listen."

The way his eyes look beyond my exterior—the way they bore into my soul—makes me uneasy and self-conscious. The words he speaks seem like a message crafted just for me. Does he know about my gifts? Can he sense something just by looking at me?

"Let me give you a boost, Mitzy." Jacob circles around and helps me into the saddle. Then he swings into his like a Wild West cowboy and tells Nimkii we'll be back in an hour.

The Native American proprietor nods solemnly and walks into his establishment.

Starlight's hooves splash into the deep puddles dotting the trail leading to Diane's trailer. Both horses slog along without hesitation and I marvel at the multitude of colors and smells surrounding me in the glittering damp forest. The leaves are changing in earnest now and the golden oranges, burnt siennas, and crimson hues draw my full attention.

As soon as we enter the clearing, I feel it. Something isn't right.

"Trailer's gone." My father's voice is quiet but concerned.

I give my mount a little kick and call to my father, "It's not gone." I manage to get Starlight to stop as I hop down, sliding precariously in the wet meadow grass. I move toward the still smoldering remains. My father's damp footsteps squeak and squish as he approaches. "Someone burned it to the ground," I whisper.

"Get back on your horse, Mitzy. We need to get out of here."

"It's all right, Dad. Whoever did this is long gone."

"What do you mean? How can you possibly know that?" He puts a hand on my arm.

"I just do, okay? Let's look around—and make sure Diane wasn't in the trailer when it happened." Why am I suggesting we look for something I absolutely do not want to find?

My father's hand slips off my arm and we circle in opposite directions around the carnage.

I'm glad I swapped out my flip-flops for tennis shoes when we stopped by the apartment to grab my hoodie. I pick up a fallen branch and poke through the charred debris.

"I don't see any human remains." Jacob's voice carries notes of relief and hope.

"Maybe she was kidnapped," I propose. "Maybe whoever killed Walt thought she knew something."

"We're not even sure what Walt was into. What makes you think Diane would've known anything about his dealings?"

"Call it daughterly intuition. If Walt was the most important person in Diane's life, I find it hard to believe she had no idea what kind of trouble he was dealing."

"Well, if someone kidnapped her, maybe the sheriff can ping her phone or something."

I flick a large piece of melted plastic siding over and stop dead in my tracks. "I don't think that's going to be possible."

My dad hurries to my side. "Is it Diane?"

"No. It's her phone."

"Speaking of phones, we better call this in. The sheriff needs to get a team out here." My dad reaches for his phone. "No reception."

I stoop over and pick up Diane's phone. I press the home key and tap in a six-digit code. The phone unlocks.

"How did you do that? Is that some kind of millennial thing?" Jacob leans toward the phone in my hand.

Turning slowly, I stare at my dad's face. At first I don't see him clearly. It's almost like I'm looking through water and he's on the other side of the swirling liquid. He snaps into focus and I look from his face to the phone and back up. "I have no idea. I think I heard the numbers—somehow." I check the recent calls and the name at the top of the list is "Ivy." "The last call she made was to her mom."

"That doesn't seem suspicious. I'm sure she was letting her know about Walt's death."

"But everyone said Ivy left Diane behind. Walt raised her on his own. How would Diane even know how to get a hold of her unless . . ."

"Unless what?" Jacob stares anxiously. "I'm starting to recognize that look. What are you think-ing, Mitzy?"

"I'm thinking either Diane was an accomplice in her father's murder or she's about to be the next victim."

Without another word, Jacob scoops me back onto my horse and sets a fast pace toward Chez Os-prey. I find myself bouncing along and hanging on for dear life.

We thunder up behind the restaurant. My dad leaps off his horse in one smooth move and runs in through the back door to the kitchen.

A moment later he returns with Nimkii in tow.

They're arguing about something. My father points to me. Nimkii points to me. My father throws his hands up in exasperation. Nimkii goes back inside and returns with a shotgun and a handgun.

My dad looks at me and shakes his head.

I carefully disentangle myself from the saddle and walk toward the pair. "So, what's going on here?"

My father crosses his strong arms over his broad chest. "He thinks we should race over to the other side of the island and see if we can find Diane before the smugglers take her to Canada."

Nimkii turns to me with his calm retort. "And your father thinks I am a foolish child who acts impulsively and without the blessings of Mother Earth."

I have no interest in getting in the middle of it, so I withhold my opinion.

Nimkii holds the handgun out for me to see as he points and explains. "This is the safety. Hold the gun in your dominant hand, lay a finger alongside the trigger, and rest that hand in the palm of the other hand. Like this." He demonstrates. "You use this sight here, and when you have the target between these two marks, pull the trigger. The clip holds thirteen rounds." He hands me the gun, grip first. "The safety is on."

With an audible swallow, I take the gun. A quick look at my dad does nothing to calm my racing heart. I shove the cold steel against my back and under the waistband of my jeans.

Jacob's ferociously chewing the inside of his cheek and shaking his head almost imperceptibly.

"I have actually shot a gun before, Dad. I grew up in Arizona. Remember? Sure, some of my foster families were new-age, patchouli-wearing hippies, but some were good ol' redneck cowboys. I may not be a deadeye shot, but I can probably provide some cover fire." For a split second there's a glimmer of pride in Jacob's eyes, before it's replaced with fatherly concern.

"No one is taking any risks today. Nimkii called it in. The sheriff is mobilizing a team. We're just going to observe and report. Everybody understand?" He waits until we respond.

My Native American gun handler and I both nod.

Nimkii saddles up a large paint named Biscuit and leads the way across the island.

The colorful trees hold no magic for me on this trip.

The weather takes a turn for the worse as Nimkii guides us through the dense woodland. Any semblance of a trail has long since disappeared. If my father and I had tried to make it across the island on our own, we would have gotten hopelessly lost.

The rain pelts down in sheets and I'm reminded of the monsoon season back in Arizona. Of course, the loamy, dark soil of the island absorbs the water nearly as fast as it falls. No danger of a flash flood here.

The lead horse stops.

"Once we reach the twisted pine tree, we'll have to leave the horses. It's only a short walk to the top of the bluff. But we want to stay out of sight of their lookouts." Nimkii gives Biscuit a little kick and we resume our silent and soggy trek.

Eventually, I feel water seeping through my jeans from the wet saddle beneath. Just when I thought things couldn't get more uncomfortable.

Nimkii signals for us to stop and he and my father hop off their mounts with ease.

I fumble around and catch my hoodie on the saddle horn as I struggle to climb down from Starlight's back. Hooked like an old jacket, I dangle with my feet still inches from the slippery, wet ground.

Jacob hurries over, unhooks me, and sets me on my feet as though I'm a small child.

Nimkii takes my horse and lashes it to a thick birch tree just out of sight.

"No more talking beyond this point. When I give you the signal to stay down"—he pushes his hand toward the earth—"stay as low as you can. All right?"

I nod.

"Whatever you say." My dad looks at me. "You sure you want to keep going?"

"Yeah, I'm sure." I don't feel sure. I feel like I have a large gun stuck in the back of my waistband and I wish it wasn't there. I also feel wet and miserable. But the thought of what might happen to Diane if we don't at least slow the smugglers down . . . I'm willing to press on.

The three of us move forward in solemn single file.

Jacob carefully holds branches out of the way for me, but the tangled mess of raspberry vines twisting across the forest floor on this side of the island is not as thoughtful. The sharp thorns scratch into the flesh beneath my jeans. Geez! And I thought all the needle-covered plants in the desert were dangerous.

Nimkii gives the signal for us to stay low.

A moment later, the silence is replaced with the sound of boats, a woman shouting orders, and gunfire.

Jacob pushes me into the mud and covers me with his body.

Nimkii crawls over to us and whispers, "Not gunfire. Backfire."

Jacob helps me to a low squat and quietly offers an apology.

The cold mud actually soothes my scratched legs, so why complain?

When we finally reach the edge of the bluff, Nimkii leads the way into a well-hidden lookout behind two huge granite boulders.

From our vantage point, we can see a flurry of activity on the rocky beachfront.

Five small speedboats tug against their anchors in a partially hidden cove. A little boat swerves between the others, with its engine coughing, spitting, and backfiring as it struggles against the waves.

Three collapsible yurts, covered with tree branches for camouflage, stand on the shore and could serve as temporary storage or sleeping quarters.

Most of the smugglers must be in one of them. Other than the pilot of the noisy motorized craft, only two men can be seen paddling a canoe out to the nearest boat, and a lone woman stands on shore with a clipboard.

The hairs on the back of my neck tingle. There's something strangely familiar about the woman. We're probably three or four hundred yards away, but something about her hair . . .

I creep closer to Jacob and tug his arm. He slips back from the lookout and gazes at me questioningly.

We're not supposed to talk, so I look around until I find a thick twig. I try to write in the mud, but my scratchings are illegible.

He leans in and pushes back my hood. His voice is a low whisper in my ear. "What?"

I follow suit and lean my lips next to his ear. "That woman is Diane."

His head whips towards me and narrowly misses my cheekbone. I lean back and fall—you guessed it—on my rear end into the mud.

Jacob reaches for Nimkii, taps him furiously, and signals him to pull back. We move as fast as we can in a low crouch and remain silent until we get back to where we tied up the horses.

Nimkii loosens the reins and we hastily mount up and ride into the protective cover of the dense forest.

Once we're a safe distance from the smuggler's cove, Nimkii halts and looks at my dad. "What is it?"

"I think we got played. That woman on the beach is Diane. She doesn't look like a victim to me."

"I'll ride back and warn the sheriff." Without so much as a "by your leave," Nimkii digs his heels into Biscuit's sides and disappears in a pounding of hooves and splattering mud.

I look at Jacob. "Can you get us back?"

He nods. "Probably."

By the time we find our way back to Chez Osprey, Sheriff Erick, Deputy Paulsen, and four uniformed officers I've never met are huddled inside the stable.

At the sound of our horses approaching, Deputy Paulsen pulls her gun.

"Easy Paulsen. That's Jacob and Mitzy." Nimkii shakes his head and quickly sidles up next to me. I attempt to hide my surprise as he slips the gun out of my waistband while he helps me climb down from Starlight's saddle.

"Let me take that horse for you, Mitzy." He leads our mounts to the stable and I'm sure there's a soft thunk of a gun being hidden at the bottom of the feed bucket.

Jacob and I approach the tight knot around the sheriff to share our news about Diane.

Sheriff Harper turns and examines me from head to muddy shoes. "Did you fall off your horse, Moon?" His smile touches his eyes and he chuckles softly.

Jacob steps up and takes control of the discussion. "Look Sheriff, I don't know what Diane and her mom are up to. But both of them seem like solid suspects."

Erick shakes his head. "When I got the call from Nimkii about the burned-up trailer and Diane possibly being kidnapped, I gave Odell a quick call to see if he had any information about Walt's other businesses. Any possible enemies."

I chime in to support my dad. "Well, we just saw Diane. She didn't get kidnapped. Looks like she's running the whole thing down there."

Erick steps away from his other officers and lowers his voice. "That's just it. Odell gave me the only number he had for Diane and told me to let her know about Walt. I called her yesterday to let her know about Walt's death. She headed back to college a week after the Pin Cherry Festival. Apparently, she attends the University of Minnesota down on the Minneapolis campus." Erick shakes his head. "So I don't know who was at that trailer, or who that woman was on the beach—but it sure as heck can't be Diane."

My knees get a little wobbly and I look up at my dad. "Whose phone did we find?"

Erick's head snaps in my direction. "You found a phone?"

I feel around inside my hoodie and pull out the phone I believed belonged to Diane. "We thought it was Diane's phone. The last number called was 'Ivy.'" I hand the phone over. "Maybe it belongs to whoever burned down the trailer?" I can't very well tell Erick that the tingling prickle running through the hairs on the back of my neck confirms my suspicion, but they do.

He takes the phone and presses the home key. "It's locked." He looks at me. "Was it unlocked when you found it?"

I have absolutely no intention of telling Sheriff Harper about my visions, feelings, or voices. "Mmhmm."

My dad arches an eyebrow.

"Paulsen, get this phone back to headquarters and see if they got a way to crack the code."

"10-4 Sheriff." Deputy Paulsen yanks an evidence bag out of her back pocket, bags the phone, seals it, and snarls in my direction. "You probably wiped any useful prints off the evidence, amateur." She brushes past me with a purposeful shoulder shove.

Outwardly I school my features to the portrait of innocence, but inwardly I smirk knowingly. Maybe I did mess up the prints, but it was worth it to get that peek at the recent calls.

Jacob puts a protective arm around me and announces, "Mitzy and I are gonna head back to the mainland. Looks like you guys have this under control."

As we hurry back to the boat, he whispers, "We better have a chat with Odell."

I nod fervently and try to ignore the squish squish of my feet in my soggy tennis shoes.

CHAPTER 14

AFTER A SHIVERY BOAT ride and a bumpy drive in my dad's F100 pickup, the dried mud on my jeans is itch-tastically unbearable. I beg Jacob to drop me off at the apartment so I can take a quick shower before we go to Myrtle's Diner.

I make it two steps inside the front door of the bookshop before Twiggy's commanding voice bellows from the back room. "Take off the wet shoes."

Don't ask me how she knows, but I have no intention of disobeying a direct order from my mission-critical volunteer employee. I slip off the wet tennis shoes and tiptoe on my mushy socks.

A loud exhale and the endless spinning of the paper towel dispenser echo from the back room.

I hop over the "No Admittance" chain, circle up the wrought-iron staircase, and rush into the apartment to avoid confrontation. However, before the bookcase door can even slide shut behind me, my Ghost-ma is all over me.

"What happened to you? You are in a state! Did you fall off your horse?"

What is it with everyone thinking I don't know how to ride a horse? I'm pretty sure I performed above average, but I don't have time to debate the finer points of my equine skills. "I need to take a shower and meet Dad at the diner."

Grams swooshes in behind me. "Not before you fill me in on the details of your muddy escapades."

I left the wet slicker on the boat for future adventures, so I start by peeling off my slightly damp hoodie. It proves an ineffective signal.

"What did Diane say? Did she cooperate?"

"Grams, I have to shower. Shoo! I'll fill you in after I've decontaminated myself."

Grams vanishes in an angry sparkle.

Turns out, it's far more difficult to remove wet, muddy skinny jeans than you may have imagined. After a great deal of tugging, wiggling, and unladylike exclamations, I am finally free of the filthy denim. I drag myself into the shower and regret that I don't have time to fully enjoy the luscious steamy water. However, I rapidly change my mind as the hot water brutally stings the raspberry-thorn scratches on my legs. I wash my hair in haste and leap out of the shower like a cat who fell into a swimming pool. I yank on clean undergarments and call for Grams to return. As I fluff my hair into a publicly acceptable shape and apply the bare minimum of makeup, I bring her up to speed on the "Diane is not Diane" dilemma.

"Well I never! Who do you think that woman is?"

"That's what we're hoping Odell can figure out."

A jarring thud comes from the bedroom, drawing both Grams and me out of the bathroom.

The ever-helpful Pyewacket has knocked a photo album off the bookshelf.

"Pye! Bad kitty! Bad!" I shake my finger in his general direction.

He grooms his whiskers as though he hasn't a care in the world.

Grams swirls toward him. "It's all right my sweet kitty," she coos as she drags her ghost fingers down his spine.

I crouch to collect the album, and admonish Grams. "Stop spoiling him. I'm the one who has to deal with his moods and his acting out when he doesn't get his way. I can't begin to imagine the indulgent life that cat had before you crossed over."

Grams chuckles. "It's not all that different from your life now, honey."

My hands hang in midair and I stop collecting the photographs that have spilled from the plastic pages and stare at my ghostly grandmother. She's right. I literally had all of this handed to me on a silver platter. Sure, I survived losing my mother and some pretty awful foster homes, but I've hardly put in more than two decades on this planet and now I've inherited a fortune. Maybe I should follow my dad's example and set up some kind of philanthropic foundation. I look up and Grams is nodding furiously.

"Re-ow." Informative, perhaps even an agreement.

"Yes, Pye. I've discovered your exhibit and I understand you're upset that we were ignoring you. Come over here and let me scratch you between the ears. Will that make things better?"

Pyewacket slinks across the floor with the abject superiority only felines can display and rubs his head against my knee—aggressively.

He knocks me off balance, the album falls, and more pictures slide out. "Geez Louise!" I set the album on the floor and begin collecting the scattered images a second time.

"REE-ow!" That one sounds dangerous.

I used to be able to ignore his outbursts, but there is something important in that missive. I stop what I'm doing and stare at the photographs spilled across the floor. I can't quite place the era, but there are several pictures featuring a hand-carved sign for the Walleye Inn and Tavern. "Grams is this Walt?"

She floats over my shoulder. "Yes, honey, that's Walter."

He looks nothing like my discovery on Boiler-plate Beach. I pull the photo closer and my mouth goes dry. "Grams. That's her."

"Her, who?"

"The woman who's not Diane. The woman on the beach, running the smuggling operation."

"Oh my stars." Grams anxiously flickers in and out.

"You know her? You actually know this woman." I tap my finger on the face in the picture.

"That's Ivy. That's Walt's ex-wife, Ivy Lapointe," she whispers.

"The woman does not age. She looked exactly like this when we saw her at the trailer. If this was taken before Diane was born . . . She must be nearly fifty now," I whisper. Dropping to my backside, I stare at the picture, and then tilt my head to get a better look at the furry fiend who made this mess. "I'm beginning to suspect this wasn't an accident, Robin Pyewacket Goodfellow."

Grams giggles in spite of my severe tone. "I always loved it when Silas called him that."

I stand and tuck the photo in the back pocket

of my jeans. I grab a tank top from the floor, make sure it's right side out, and slip it on. This one says, "Roses are Dead. Violets are blew." and there's a stick of dynamite in the violet. What can I say? I went through an anti-love phase in my late teens.

Donning my simple flip-flops, I walk to the diner, ignoring the sputter of raindrops intent on testing my tolerance.

Good ol' Johan Olafsson drives his tractor down Main Street without a care in the world. I wave happily. Every time I see that guy, I remember how much he annoys Deputy Paulsen and I regret she can't see him in action right now.

Inside the nearly empty restaurant, I find Odell and my father with their heads close together across the table in the back corner booth. I approach slowly. My dad is the first to look up.

"Hey Mitzy. You're not going to believe what Odell told me."

With both hands resting on the table, I tilt my head and say, "Let me guess. The woman we thought was Diane—the woman we saw running the smuggling operation—it was Ivy Lapointe."

Jacob and Odell stare at me like I have two heads.

"Now, how in the Sam Hill do you know that?" says Odell.

I extract the photo from my back pocket and slap it down in the middle of the table.

Odell takes one look at it and let's out a long low whistle. "I ain't seen this photo for twenty years. You find this at the trailer?"

While part of me is anxious to take full credit, I feel I would be remiss if I didn't let the gentlemen know the intricate part my cat played in discovering the helpful picture. "Actually, the one and only Pyewacket knocked a photo album off the book-shelves and scolded me until I found this in the mess on the floor."

Jacob shakes his head and exhales. "That cat has always given me the creeps. It's like he thinks he's human. He looks at you like he knows things."

"Always? How long has Grams had Pyewack-et?" I ask.

My dad looks up and to the left. "Hmmm, I can't remember him not being around. She must've gotten him when I was too little to notice—maybe even before I was born."

I narrow my gaze. "You must be mistaken. Cats don't live forty plus years!"

Jacob shrugs. "They do when they're spoiled beyond all reason."

Odell picks up the photo and rubs his thumb over the face of his brother. "I let you down, Walt. I let you down and I'm real sorry."

Anxious to move away from the heavy emotion, I volunteer my theory. "I think Ivy killed Walt. Maybe she killed Lars too."

"Do we actually know if Lars is dead?" Jacob squints his eyes and leans back.

"Lars Gershon?" Odell looks from me to my dad and back to me again.

"Yeah, Sheriff Erick found his business card near Walt's body. He thought I dropped it, so he returned it to me. I called to follow up on it yesterday and his assistant was pretty upset. She had just gotten a call about an hour before. Lars is definitely dead."

The door of the diner scrapes open and Sheriff Erick hustles into the room. "Should've known I'd find you three scheming."

I throw a hand on my curvy hip and reply, "I've never schemed a day in my life, Erick."

Sadly, I am woefully unprepared for the guffaws that erupt from Jacob and Odell. In fact, the delectable local sheriff adds a chuckle of his own.

"Wow. Just, wow." I stare daggers at the three of them.

Odell slides out of the red vinyl booth and straightens his grease-stained apron. "You just checking up on us, Sheriff? Or you got something to report?"

"I have a possible ID on the woman—"

"Ivy Lapointe," I blurt.

Erick's shoulders deflate and he shakes his head. "How do you do that?" There is a lovely hint of admiration in his eyes.

This time I kick the meddling Pyewacket to the proverbial curb and take full credit. "It's a gift." I get a tingle on my bare ring finger. I didn't realize how much of the truth I was actually telling.

"We're still looking into how Walt's tied up in this whole mess. The actual Diane wasn't able to provide much information. She said she'll come up from college tomorrow and give us whatever she has on her mother, but it doesn't sound like much. They've been estranged almost Diane's whole life."

I can't imagine a mother not wanting her own child. It was hard enough for me to cope with my mother being taken from me by a tragedy. I don't think I would've been able to hold it together if she had straight up abandoned me. I keep my thoughts to myself and slide into the booth next to my dad.

"Hungry?" Odell winks in my direction.

"As ever," I shamelessly reply.

He heads back to the kitchen and the familiar sounds of burgers sizzling on the grill and fries bubbling in hot oil fill me with joyous anticipation. I can't imagine a better smell than freshly fried potatoes! With the possible exception of freshly fried potatoes being fed to me by the crisp, slightly woodsy smelling Sheriff Erick!

"Is there anything else you're forgetting to tell me, Moon?" He takes a step closer.

Startled back to the present, I hope and pray that Erick can't read my mind, and I'm about to say no, when I remember Lars Gershon. "It might interest you to know that Lars Gershon is also dead."

Erick raises an eyebrow, shakes his head, but eventually nods. "We got a call from Lake County first thing this morning." He tilts his head and grins as he adds, "But I appreciate you keeping me in the loop." He hooks a thumb over his Sam Browne belt and I am powerless to prevent my eyes from following the gesture toward his thinly concealed abs.

Jacob hits me square on the floating rib with an elbow jab.

I pop my eyes up like a schoolgirl busted by the principal and blurt, "Thanks for stopping by, Erick."

He hesitates for a minute and I'm not sure if his expression is confusion or hurt. "I better be gettin' back to the station." He nods to the table in general and walks out without a backward glance.

Which is fortunate, because if he had looked back, I would've gotten busted a second time.

CHAPTER 15

BRIGHT AND EARLY the next morning—which is around 9:00 AM for me—and armed with the photo of Ivy Lapointe, I take a little drive south to Gershon Antiquities in my sporty silver Mercedes 300SL coupe with gullwing doors.

The trees at this latitude include a wider variety of species and are starting to melt from bright greens to light yellows. But if the local gossip is to be believed, when autumn hits its stride up here in the great North, the rainbow of colors will be breathtaking. I'm actually looking forward to it after the palette-teaser on the island. There's a lot more vegetation in Sedona than people assume, but most of the trees are some version of pine so the fall-color display is a little less spectacular.

I have to remember to ask Grams about

Pyewacket. I have a hard time believing my dad's version of that story. A forty-year-old cat! I don't think so, Dad. The city limits sign for Grand Falls races into view and I check my phone for the final directions to the antique store.

After parking on the near empty street, I'm stunned to discover Gershon Antiquities is not so much an antique store as a dealer who specializes in high-end private collections.

"Welcome to Gershon Antiquities. How may I help you?"

That's definitely the southern drawl from the telephone. "Hi, I called earlier about Lars. I'm so sorry for your loss. I'm Isadora Duncan's granddaughter." I secretly hope that name carries as much weight as my dad believes it does.

The petite redhead scurries out from behind her immaculate Louis XVI desk and shuffles over as fast as her snug, narrow pencil skirt will allow. "So nice to make your acquaintance. I'm so sorry I hung up on you." She puts a hand to her forehead. "Where were my manners?" The hand drops to her side and rubs the fabric of her skirt. "I was just so flabbergasted by the news about Mr. Gershon. I hadn't had a chance to collect myself. Again, I'm so sorry, Miss—"

"Mitzy Moon. Isadora is my paternal grandmother." Not sure why I felt the need to add that, but I will definitely remove it from my future repertoire. If my extensive background in film and television has taught me anything, I need to walk around this establishment and search for hidden clues, and I need to get her talking. "That is a gorgeous desk." I gesture to her previous perch.

"Oh, isn't it a divine desk? I just adore French antiques. There was a famous firm in Paris, Maison Jansen, which just made the most wonderful items. This exquisite little writing table is custom-made solid walnut, with silver leaf mirrored *verre églomisé*, reverse painting. And it's in perfect condition! They don't make pieces from solid quarter-sawn oak with lovely dove-tailed construction like this anymore."

I bite my tongue. Apparently, it's not that hard to get her talking. I didn't understand a word of that diatribe, other than "desk."

"Are you looking for something in particular, Miss Moon?"

"I feel like I'll know it when I see it. My grandmother's taste was rather eclectic, and I'm looking to continue that theme in the decor." I can almost see the character I'm playing. Maybe a mid-1990s Michelle Pfeiffer? Or perhaps an early-2000s Nicole Kidman? I throw myself into the role. I study each piece as though my life could depend on purchasing it.

"That vase is a lovely addition to any home. It's from a large estate sale we coordinated out on the island. Most of the items were what we like to call 'hunting lodge chic,' but there were a few high-value pieces that we brought into our collection."

An estate sale on the island? I can't imagine smugglers selling off their goods so publicly. Chez Osprey seemed completely intact. She can't possibly mean . . .

"If you're interested in any jewelry, let me know. I have a private room with special lighting and a large mirror."

Keep it general. Don't pounce, I tell myself. "I'd love to see the jewelry."

She leads me into a small room off to the side where a three-tiered glass jewelry case glows with precious gemstones. The pin lighting bounces off the exquisite stones and casts a tantalizing sparkle against the walls and ceiling. It almost makes me want to buy some jewelry.

"Where do you get these wonderful pieces?"

"I'm sure you know there's an aging population this far north of the big city. People move up here to get some peace and quiet in their golden years, and many of them don't have close relatives. Some of the sales come during their lifetime to finance home repairs or bucket-list trips, but a great deal of our stock comes in through our estate sales."

"Like the one out on the island?"

"Oh yes, but that was what we call a 'live one'."
She giggles into her hand.

I have to ask. I can't possibly contain my question any longer. "Oh that's devilish. What does that mean?"

She blanches and lets a self-conscious gasp escape her thin lips. "I shouldn't have said that."

"Nonsense. It's just us girls. You can tell me."
Now I feel like every mean girl in every high school movie that has ever been made.

"Oh, all right. We call it a 'live one' when someone sells off their estate before they die. This man was in a huge hurry to unload not only his quality items, but he wanted us to get rid of everything."

"Oh that seems beneath you." I shake my head and pretend to understand.

She tiptoes closer and puts a hand on her chest. "I know! Right? We're designed to deal with high-end items. I can assure you I've never before had to find a home for a singing trout on a plaque."

I'm not sure how I prevent myself from blurting that it was probably a walleye—from Walleye Lodge. But she's said enough to convince me that the "estate sale on the island" was held by Walt Johnson. Now I found my connection; all I need is a motive.

"Were there any other dealers helping you sell off his items?"

"It's so funny you should ask. We rarely split commissions, but as I mentioned some of the lower-end items just didn't fit with our clientele. So we partnered with a pawnshop"—she whispers the last two words and shakes her head indignantly before continuing—"over in Round Rock. I'm sure they did great with their part of the inventory."

"Do they pay you a finder's fee or something?"

She looks at me as though I've just grown horns. Her southern accent takes on an edge. "Are you with the police?"

"Hardly! I'm just nosy." I fake chuckle as long as I possibly can and feign interest in a few baubles.

I'm about to leave when a section of military pins and medals catch my interest. "Are these from the estate sale on the island?"

She leans in and whispers, "Honestly, I should've sent them to Round Rock. But Lars, God rest him, insisted."

"I'll take 'em."

"Which ones?" She eyes me suspiciously.

"All of them." I strut out of the pretentious side room and up to the register, waiting for her to catch up.

She scurries after me with her tight-kneed mermaid waddle, carrying the tray of medals. "I'll ring these up for you right away, Miss Moon."

I swallow my glee. "Can you gift wrap the whole tray? I'll pay whatever extra for that." That'll teach her to judge a baby-face chick in skinny jeans. I might not look the part, but I'm loaded. Clearly, I say none of this aloud.

She hands me a lovely golden package tied with a silver ribbon.

I take my purchase back to the car and stew over this new information. I know Walt was in financial trouble, so the estate sale makes perfect sense. But what if there's more to it? Erick said something about Diane coming up from college. I need to make sure Odell introduces us.

I'm tempted to drive to Round Rock and question the pawnbroker, but my stomach is anxious to get back to the diner. For a couple of reasons.

I wave to Odell as I enter the diner and he throws down a burger.

"Hey, Tally, how's business?" I ask.

She glances around the room and her snug flaming-red bun holds firm on top of her head. "Looks like you're it, Mitzy."

I chuckle and take a seat.

"You want pop or coffee?"

I snicker at the northern expression and reply, "I'll have a soda. Thanks."

She nods and hustles behind the counter to re-trieve my beverage.

I pull out my phone to look through my notes. Found Walt's body Monday morning. Talked to Diane—I delete Diane and type Ivy. Talked to Ivy on Tuesday. Heard about Lars Gershon's death on Tuesday. I set my phone on the table and lean back. With my eyes closed I replay my first visit to the burned-out site of the former Walleye Lodge.

The woman's long black hair definitely gave her a youthful appearance, but why did we assume she was Diane? I guess Jacob assumed it was Diane and I simply followed his lead. No. She introduced her-self as Diane and my dad didn't argue. But he prob-ably hasn't seen Diane in more than fifteen years. It could be pretty easy to mistake the remembered face of a five-year-old girl for the transformed face of the woman living in a trailer next to the de-stroyed lodge that used to belong to her father. I study the image of the woman's face in my mind. Now I recall the lines around her eyes. Little lines around her mouth. A crease between her eyebrows and the mole on her left cheek. There were subtle signs of age, but for the most part time has been kind to Ivy Lapointe. Fifty might be the new thirty, but not many women her age could pass for a twenty-year-old.

That tattoo! That was no tribute to a missing

mother. That tattoo of ivy on Ivy's arm—talk about on the nose—is probably what inspired the tattoo of "ivy" on Walt's mermaid's arm. It's tattoo *Inception!*

Odell sets my plate on the table and slides in the bench seat across the table from me. "Seems like that little brain a yours might blow a gasket." He chuckles and interlaces his fingers, twirling his thumbs absently. "You find out anything about Walt today?"

The image of Ivy evaporates and I reach down to the package on the seat next to me. I push the present across the table toward Odell.

"What's this? It ain't my birthday."

"Just open it."

He rips into the gold tissue paper and stops as soon as he exposes the Purple Heart. His fingers reach down and tenderly rub the medal. "Where did you get this?" he breathes.

"I paid a visit to Gershon Antiquities today. I discovered Walt had a big estate sale. And I'd have to say that sale must've been before the fire."

Odell looks up at me, his face a swirl of confusion, disbelief, and anger. "Can't believe he sold off my grandpa's medals!" He shakes his head. "I'm not sure how he got his hands on them in the first place."

"How much do you know about the fire that destroyed Walt's lodge?"

Odell runs his fingers across a few more pieces of his grandfather's military legacy before leaning back and letting a heavy sigh escape his chest. "Not much, kid. Like I told you before—I cut Walt off. I told him I wasn't bailing him out anymore and that was pretty much the last I heard from him. 'Course, it's a small town and I heard about the fire, but once I learned Walt was all right, I just let it lie." He leans forward and rests his elbows on the table. "Why do you ask?"

"Something tells me it wasn't an accident."

"Well, he'd a been a bigger fool than I imagined if he burned down that place without having any insurance."

"I'm not entirely sure Walt burned it down. And I've also got a pretty solid feeling that it wasn't an insurance scam."

Odell tilts his head and fixes me with a puzzled stare. "What are you cooking up over there?"

"Don't you find it strange that Walt sold everything he had that was of any value, and apparently some things that weren't even his, before the fire? I mean, doesn't that seem a little too convenient?"

"I see your point. But if there was no money in it, why burn it down?"

I nod, but push my idea. "Maybe it was a warning. Maybe he got in with the wrong people and they were trying to scare him, for some reason." I chew on the inside of my cheek and add, "Walt must've suspected something was up . . . Or maybe he was trying to raise enough money to pay them off?"

"I guess it makes about as much sense as anything else. But Walt's gone. It's not like you can confirm your theory."

This is exactly the conversational opportunity I was hoping for but don't want to jump in too quickly and lose my chance. "I thought you might introduce me to Diane, when she comes up this weekend."

Odell slides out of the booth with a chuckle and raps his knuckles on the table before he walks back to the kitchen. "Whatever you need, kid. Whatever you need." He sighs and the metal spatula scraping across the grill signals the end of our discussion.

I'm not stupid enough to think I outsmarted him, but I am pleased he's going to allow me to play through. Now it's time for me to mosey on over to the police station and see if I can't continue my winning streak and weasel a few more answers from Erick.

Just as soon as I finish my fries . . .

• • •

The uniformed officer obsessed with the Furious Monkeys app has a pint-sized sidekick—a curly-haired child of five or possibly ten. I have no idea why. The police station is fairly quiet, but as I scan the room it becomes clear that there's been an invasion of Mini-Mes. I approach the counter and give the small girl a wave. "Is it 'take your mom to work' day?"

The little girl giggles and looks away.

Her mother does not look up from her phone.

The little girl's eyes widen and she stares at my white-blonde hair. "Why did you cut your hair, Elsa?"

I shake my head. "I don't think we've met. I'm Mitzy Moon."

At that pronouncement, Furious Monkeys puts down her phone. "Here to see the sheriff?"

"I sure am."

The little girl leans toward her mother and whispers, "Why does Elsa want to see the sheriff? Is she in trouble for turning someone into ice?"

The mother looks at me and for the first time actually seems to realize I am a human standing across from her in this reality. She stares at my hair and chuckles. I wish I could say it's the first time I've endured that reaction.

She turns to her daughter and announces,

"That's no Disney princess, sweetheart. In fact, just last month she was accused of murder."

The little girl gasps. "Don't worry, Elsa, your sister will save you."

For some unknown reason, that innocent phrase gets me right in the gut. I swallow hard and blink back unwelcome emotions. I borrow Odell's term of endearment. "Thanks, kid." Shifting my attention back to the mother, I ask, "Is Erick in his office?"

Furious Monkeys has already returned to the world inside her phone and nods without looking up. I sashay through the swinging gate and find my way to my next quarry.

Erick looks up as I enter and quickly closes the folder in front of him. "Do you have something to tell me?"

Don't worry, I got a peek in the folder before he flipped it shut. He was studying a report with a Coast Guard seal at the top for some reason. The neat, orderly printing caught my attention. I refrain from answering his direct question and instead help myself to an uncomfortable seat in his dilapidated office chair. "I feel like I've already given you quite a bit, Erick. It's time you shared a thing or two with me."

His rolly office chair squeaks as he leans back. "Is that so?"

Seems like he's in a fairly decent mood, so I

push on. "Can you tell me about the fire that burned down Walt Johnson's tavern?"

He hesitates and slides the folder in front of him underneath a stack to his left. "What's got you so interested in that fire? It was months ago."

"Were there a lot of personal effects lost in the fire?"

He leans forward. "That's an odd question, Moon. Walt was living in the owner's quarters when the place burned down and his daughter was at school. It stands to reason they had personal effects in those rooms, doesn't it?"

Two can play this game. "Does it?"

His eyes twinkle as he replies, "Has anyone ever told you you're an infuriating woman?"

I lean back and laugh heartily. "If I had a quarter for every time someone said that. Well, I'd be—oh, that's right, I am."

He shakes his head. "The fire happened at the tail end of winter—almost spring. We had a huge, unseasonably late snowfall this year, and the fire marshal wouldn't send anyone out to the island. He said there was no way to get a sufficient water supply with everything still pretty iced over and that dispatching a helicopter would be a waste of funds. He took one look at the color of the smoke and said it looked like an accelerant had been used. He figured the deep snow surrounding the lodge would prevent the fire from spreading and he made the call to let it burn out. We'd already confirmed that Walt had gotten out safely."

I ponder the details carefully and find the timing of the blaze and the deep snowfall a little too convenient. "The fire was in April?"

"Early on, if I remember correctly."

I nod and lean toward his irresistible jawline. "And when did you realize who had set the fire?"

"I don't know who set the fire, Moon. Maybe no one. There was no insurance policy, no insurance claim, and no investigation. What are you getting at?"

I put my hand on the desk and tap my fingers. "That's some real shoddy police work, Erick. I spent some time at Gershon Antiquities today and learned that Walt had a massive estate sale in late March, before the fire. *Right* before the fire. Doesn't that strike you as odd?"

He avoids making eye contact and leans away from my tapping fingers. "There's no telling what that guy was up to. What are you getting at?"

"What I'm getting at is that whoever burned down the lodge was sending Walt a message. Maybe he sold off all his possessions because he needed money. He couldn't sell the lodge because he owed more than it was worth and he was using it as collateral for his boats. He couldn't burn it down for insurance money because he let the insurance lapse. Maybe someone burned it down in an attempt to push him farther into a corner. They wanted to take away his options."

Erick straightens up in his chair and clenches his jaw. "You think Ivy had something to do with this? It sounds like you think she was trying to push him into the smuggling business. That right?"

I smile as I hoist myself out of the chair and walk toward the door. I turn, look over my shoulder, and give Erick a little wink. "Seems like it would be something worth looking into, Sheriff."

He grumbles something about being the one to direct the investigation.

Unable to resist, I add, "Oh, and you should ask Paulsen if that boat key belonged to the deceased."

He stands, fumbles for a comeback, and ends up with, "What key?"

I grin, raise one eyebrow, and exit.

CHAPTER 16

BACK AT THE BELL, BOOK & CANDLE everything is silent. Twiggy has gone home for the day and I've checked all the high places for any sign of Pyewacket. He's gotten the jump on me one too many times and I'm growing extra cautious. As I reach the top of the circular staircase, the beautiful tomes displayed on every desk in the Rare Books Loft surprise me. Each volume is opened to a specific page and a set of white gloves rest atop every manuscript. Tomorrow must be the monthly event that Twiggy mentioned. I've been told that my grandmother was generous with her collection—to a point. She would allow scholars and researchers from around the world to make reservations to spend a day with any volume from her rare books collection. It must be quite a sought-after appointment. There was a book on every one of the twenty-five reading desks.

I'll have to remember to put on pants before I stumble out of the apartment tomorrow morning. I reach up and grab the candle handle next to the empty spot where *Saducismus Triumphatus* usually rests and pull the lever down. The hidden bookcase door slides open with a satisfying whoosh. I step through and crash directly into a huge corkboard on wheels. "What the—?"

Grams materializes. "Watch your language, young lady."

"What the heck is this doing in the middle of my apartment?"

"I like to call it *our* apartment." She giggles. "Twiggy brought that up earlier. She announced to the room that you had requested tacks and string, but she didn't want you making any holes in the walls."

I open my mouth to protest, but then I remember that every good detective movie I've ever seen has a murder wall. I mean, sometimes it's a missing-kid wall, or a pyro wall, or a kidnapped-woman wall . . . Well, you get the idea. It's a visual place to organize my suspect list.

I rip open the package of tacks, grasp one between my thumb and forefinger, and press it through the picture of Ivy Lapointe with great satisfaction.

I step back.

Grams chuckles.

I spin around. "It's a start. Rome wasn't built in a day."

"A stitch in time saves nine. There's a hole in the bucket, dear Liza." Grams is laughing uncontrollably now.

"I don't think I like it when you use my tactics against me. Leave the sarcasm to the living."

She floats closer and puts an arm around my shoulders. I feel the tingle of her energy mixing with mine. It's not quite real; there's no weight to her presence. But there's a satisfying comfort nonetheless.

"I tease because I love, Mitzy. You are truly an amazing granddaughter and I know you can solve this case."

I wish I felt as confident as she thinks I should. I pull out the photo album that my helpful rescued caracal knocked down and thumb through all the pictures from the Walleye Lodge and Tavern. There really was a preponderance of taxidermy monstrosities in that place. But even an untrained eye like mine can see the finer pieces tucked amongst the hunting trophies and old fishing poles.

In fact, some of the elegant items look downright out of place. "Grams?"

She zooms in so quickly my heart skips a beat.

"What do you need, dear?"

"Probably a package of Depends would be handy!"

"Oh Mitzy, you're such a hoot."

"Grams, you have a lot more experience with antiques. Do you see anything in these photos that would've had some real value?"

She looks over the items and there is an occasional "Oooo" or an "Awww" and finally an "Oh my goodness!"

"What is it?"

"Well, that Bengt Nordenberg painting over the mantelpiece is worth a small fortune. And it was Cal's. I have no idea how Walt had gotten a hold of it or why it would've been placed on display at the lodge."

I take one of the index cards from the stack provided by Twiggy and write down "stolen antiques" and I pin it up on my corkboard. A few more card-worthy ideas come to mind and I also copy the notes from my phone. No matter how I attempt to arrange the cards, I can't make many solid connections between the random "leads."

"Any luck?"

"Nope. They make it look so easy in the movies. You put stuff on a board, tie some string around a few tacks, and 'bingo,' you've got your man—or woman, as the case may be." I step back and look at my arbitrary array. "Mine just looks like a really sad vision board."

With the wall of clues to my back, I pace down the row of six-by-six windows, stopping abruptly when I notice the handgun still lying on my bed. Oops! Looks like I forgot to call Sheriff Erick about that. As I walk a little closer and stare down at the pistol, another plan takes shape.

Jacob mentioned some friend of his could take me to the shooting range and teach me about guns, or something. Maybe I should just hang on to this pistol and—

"Mitzy Moon! Don't you make me use your proper name! You will do no such thing. In fact, I insist that you pick up your phone and call the sheriff immediately. You have no idea where that gun has been." Grams floats directly above the handgun and stares at me with ghostly fury until I retrieve my phone and dial the sheriff's station.

"May I speak to Sheriff Harper, please?" I stick my tongue out at the bossy apparition who is still giving me the stink eye.

Grams nods victoriously and I'm forced to look away from her pious grin.

"What? Oh, yes. You can tell him it's Mitzy

Moon." Without any further questions, my call is transferred. "Hi, Erick. It's Mitzy . . . Oh, I know. But here's the thing, Erick, I need you to come to my apartment and pick up a most-likely-unregistered gun."

There is a deafening silence on the opposite end of the call.

"Are you still there? I said, I have a gun that doesn't belong to me and I was hoping you would come and pick it up."

He explains how that's not in his job description and asks me why I don't just bring it down to the station.

"For one thing, I don't want to get my fingerprints on it. I've already been accused of murder once in this town. Lord knows what you'd try to pin on me if I pick up that gun. And the second thing —" I look at Grams and shrug.

She points wild finger guns at me and throws her hands up in the air like she's crazy.

Stifling a chuckle, I continue, "And the second thing, I don't know the first thing about guns." I smile at my grandmother and wink.

She nods with approval.

"Thank you, Erick." I end the call and update Grams. "He's on his way."

She takes a lap around the room and gasps. "What about the murder wall?"

"Oh, Humpty Dumpty!" My desperate search around the room for a place to hide a giant rolling corkboard reveals no ready-made stash room. Hopeless. I grab the thing and wheel it toward the closet, but there is no way it will fit through the door. Panic rises in my chest. It's a short walk from the sheriff's station to the bookstore.

"He'll be here any minute," shrieks Grams.

"Not helping!" I retort.

Maybe the bedspread could be thrown over the top, although that seems almost more suspicious. And with my luck the gun would fall on the floor and go off. And with even more of my luck, I'd shoot myself.

I wheel the board back toward the secret door when Grams' face pops right through the cork. I gasp and step back. "Grams! Honestly."

"You'll forgive me once you hear what I have to say." I throw my hands up and roll my eyes.

"You only have about five things tacked on the board, sweetie. Maybe just take them down."

Raising a finger to admonish her for scaring just a little bit of pee out of me—once again—I hesitate and have to admit her suggestion is actually a solid plan.

She smiles.

I hastily pull the tacks out, collect the index cards and the picture of Ivy Lapointe, and shove them in between two photo albums on the bookshelf.

My phone rings. It's him! I have to calm down. Geez! I attempt to slow my breathing before I say, "Hello?"

Erick's sexy voice caresses my eardrum. "I'm here, but the door's locked. Are you planning on letting me in?"

"Be right down." I push the panel, race down the stairs—manage to avoid tripping over the "No Admittance" chain—and unlock the front door. No matter how prepared I thought I was, the sight of Sheriff Erick posted up outside my door, back-lit by the streetlamp, is more thrilling than I care to admit.

"So where's this gun, Moon?"

"Follow me, Erick." I put a little wiggle in my waddle as I lead him upstairs. "I have to ask you to turn around, Erick. I can't reveal all my secrets on our first date."

He opens his mouth as though he might protest. Instead he shakes his head and does as he is told.

After I'm sure he's not watching, I reach up and pull the candle handle. The bookcase slides open and I announce, "You can turn around now."

Erick gives a low whistle. "Always full of surprises."

I lead him into my boudoir and tingles race over my skin. If only he were here for more than an armory related errand. "That's it over there, on the bed."

As Erick walks toward my bed, I can't resist the urge to mentally undress him, mentally put him in the bed, and mentally join him.

"Behave yourself, young lady," whispers Grams.

I shake the vision from my head and attempt to strike a professional pose.

Grams whispers in my other ear, "And what profession would that be?" Fresh snickers echo through my head.

Erick takes a pen from his front pocket, pokes it through the trigger guard, and carefully places the gun in an evidence bag. "I don't suppose you're going to tell me where you got this?"

I shrug. "I just moved in here. The cat dragged it out from under the bed. Who knows where it came from?" I hope my face looks as innocent as my voice sounds.

He shakes his head. "Unless you have any other unregistered firearms, Moon. I'll be on my way."

I had hoped he would stick around and interrogate me a little more, but it seems the presence of my bed has thrown off his law enforcement instincts. I convince myself this can only happen because he's trying to resist his powerful attraction to me. Maybe he needs a little nudge. "Are you sure you don't have time for a drink?" I giggle nervously.

He blushes the appropriate shade of pink. "I need to get back to the station. I appreciate you calling this in." He gives a gentlemanly tip of his head and walks out of my apartment.

What's that line I'm thinking of? Oh yeah, I hate to see him go, but I love to watch him leave.

A loud ghost groan comes from somewhere behind me.

"Let me know what you find out about that weapon, won't you Erick?"

His chuckle follows him down the stairs.

Eager to catch a last glimpse, I follow at a respectable distance, and lock up after he leaves.

Confident that a good night's sleep will bring clarity to my investigation into Walt Johnson's murder, I pin the photo of Ivy and my notes back on the corkboard before collapsing into bed.

Sadly, dreams of Erick elude me, and when Pyewacket pounces on my chest at the ungodly hour of 8:00 AM, I feel more relief than anger.

"Come on, buddy. Let's get you some Fruity Puffs and me some wake-up juice." I lean heavily against the plaster medallion above the intercom and yawn as the bookcase slides open.

"Great Expectations!" I slam my hand against the button a second time and twist away from the opening to hide from view while the door slides shut.

"RE-ow." The standard Threat Level Yellow version of "Feed me."

"Don't you dare start with me, Pye. The entire loft is filled with hoity-toity academics! I can't go prancing out there in my shorty jammies."

"Reow." Quiet insistence.

"Well, I vote no." Turning my back on the indignant feline, I stumble into the closet to find some socially acceptable duds.

"You always look nice in blue," enthuses Grams.

My heart thuds against my ribs. "Holy Hera, woman! I am not awake. I have not had coffee. And I've already been ogled by at least twenty book nerds!"

Grams sighs and disappears through the wall.

I grab a navy-blue T-shirt that reads, "A large group of people is called a 'no thank you,'" and a pair of black leggings. Blue and black don't really go together, you say? Tell that to Eddie Izzard.

Now armed with pants, I confidently reopen the door and stride onto the loft like I own the place. Which, of course, I do.

Stares and whispers oscillate across the loft like a brisk summer wind over a wheat field.

Teetering between offended and delighted, I pause.

An oddly familiar pair of shiny men's shoes

tickles a memory, but I'm preempted from further investigation by a low growl from Pyewacket. Before I can react, he charges down the circular staircase, darts between two rows of bookcases, and the bookshop is filled with a blood-curdling yowl.

Hurrying after him, I skitter to a halt just behind his arched back and bared fangs.

What is this guy doing in my bookshop? "Gary? You read?" That came out much more condescendingly than it sounded in my head. Dockworkers can read, he just didn't— Never mind, I'll only dig myself a deeper hole. I try another tack. "What are you doing here?"

If guilt had a signature expression, it would be the look on Gary's face. "Hey, you. I was wondering if you wanted to hook up again sometime?"

Is this guy for real? He still doesn't remember my name and he's hitting on me? I'm honestly tempted to encourage Pyewacket to maul him.

Gary swallows audibly. "Can you call off your cougar, or whatever?"

Now you get what I was saying about him not striking me as the literary type, right? I don't have time for this jerk. "Pye, wait for me in the back room or no Fruity Puffs for you."

Pyewacket drops one more insolent hiss before complying with my request.

"Seriously, what are you doing here, Gary?"

"Can't a guy buy a book?"

A quick glance at the self-help book in Gary's hands that promises to guide you to financial freedom through knitting, and I literally laugh out loud. "Don't get your yarn in a twist." My sense of humor sails over Gary's head, but let me be clear—the play on words was totally intended.

He shoves the volume in his hand back on a random shelf and takes a step toward me. "Okay, you got me. I just wanted to see you again. I don't really read."

Bingo! Before I can offer a snarky response, I hear the whispered word, "Danger." I step back and look around. There's no one else in the stacks, and no Grams hovering above us. Now I'm hearing voices? My life just keeps getting weirder. "Gary, I got a lot on my plate right now. I'm not looking for a relationship or even a two-night stand. You're nice, it was great, let's keep in touch. Buh-bye." Without waiting for his reply, I hustle into the back room and dump Fruity Puffs into Pye's bowl. Thankfully Twiggy has already brewed coffee and I eagerly pour myself a steaming mug of liquid alert.

"You're up early, doll." Twiggy clomps over to the computer, slides the mouse, and types something into an open document.

"So the book nerds upstairs, they're all researchers?"

She doesn't look up or stop typing. "They make reservations, they follow the rules. I don't ask a lot of questions."

"But—" I don't have the energy to play this game today. "Do you need help?"

She turns around slowly and cocks one eyebrow. "From you?"

I shake my head. "You're right. It was a stupid question. I'm off to find some breakfast, and see if I can't get a little more information from the sheriff before I meet Diane."

Twiggy swallows hard and crosses her arms. "You think her mom did it?"

I shrug. "I'm sure Ivy is involved. Whether she's the one who killed Walt or if she just put him in harm's way, I don't know yet." I stand up, rinse out my mug, and set it in the dish drainer. "I'll keep you in the loop. We're gonna figure out who did this."

I make it all the way past the bistro table and have one foot out the door of the back room before Twiggy says, "Thanks."

I nod and keep walking.

CHAPTER 17

THE FLAT GREY MORNING LIGHT promises nothing. After an uneventful breakfast and a "goose egg" on the boat key at the sheriff's station, I shift gears. Seems like the perfect day to go check out the pawnshop. I drive to Round Rock in no real hurry, warily watching the rough waves on the lake and the dark clouds gathering on the horizon.

Hoping to catch the pawnbroker in a chatty mood, I park my gullwing Mercedes a couple of blocks away. Wouldn't you know? Mother Nature chooses that moment to bless us with an intermittent autumn shower. By the time I push open the door beneath the three white globes, I look more like a drowned rat than an heiress.

Perfect. Actually perfect, not sarcastically.

I swipe a thumb under each eye and pull my

clingy wet T-shirt off my chest. I want the guy to talk, not gawk.

Poking around the shop, on an intense search for nothing, I finally draw the owner's attention.

"Are you looking for anything special, Miss?"

I run my fingers through my hair and wipe a little more water off my face. "I'm looking for a present for my grandmother's birthday. Do you have anything that might appeal to an older generation?" I replace the lid on the yellow, smiley-face cookie jar and grin helplessly at the shopkeeper.

He walks out from behind the counter and returns my smile. "Well, aren't you a thoughtful granddaughter. Let me see what I can find."

"She has pretty eclectic décor. A lot of antlers, and for some reason one of those singing fish on a plaque. Have you seen those things?"

He turns and shares a chuckle. "You're not gonna believe this, but a few months back, I got a whole load of stuff from a guy's place out on the island. And I'll be darned if there wasn't one of those plaques in the mix. We've sold a lot of things from that batch, but I'll show you what we have left."

Fantastic. I follow him around like an eager puppy and he shows me all manner of taxidermy and hunting-lodge décor.

"Do you have any paintings?"

The shopkeeper slaps his thigh as though I'm

the most hilarious person he's ever met. "Well, gosh darn it, you must be psychic."

He has no idea. "Oh, you're too much," I reply.

"There was one that we held against a pawn ticket. The fella needed cash and wanted to unload everything, except one painting he said he'd buy back when he could. That ticket expired a couple weeks ago and he didn't show up, so I put her out on the floor." He walks down an aisle crowded tightly with souvenir X-Men glasses, nondescript pottery, and rusty washbasins. We turn the corner, go up two steps, and pass into a space I'll refer to as "pawnshop chic."

"If I remember correctly, those three over there all came from the island—including the one from the expired ticket. But as you can see, there's quite a selection here." He raises his hands and gestures to the many horrible paintings of dogs and other animals playing poker adorning the walls. "I'll leave you here for a few minutes so you can look around."

It only takes me a moment to locate the Nordenberg. Seems like Walt purposely kept it from Lars Gershon's greedy eyes and had every intention of recovering it. I carefully lift it off the wall hook and check the price tag dangling from a crooked piece of scotch tape on the back. $75. If my grandmother is to be believed, this painting is literally worth tens of thousands, and here it is in a pawn-shop for $75. I can't believe my luck.

Stifling my glee, I meander the narrow path-ways and climb up and down some additional stairs, before returning to the front counter.

"Looks like you found something."

I smile broadly. "I sure did. This will go per-fectly in her sitting room. Thanks so much for taking the time to show me around." I carefully lay the painting on the counter.

"Oh, I'm so glad this one is finding a new home. The man who pawned it used to stop by with his pawn ticket and make sure I was still holding it for him. Each time, after he came by, I'd be tempted to make him some kind of deal. He always looked so desperate to buy it back. Then one day he stopped coming. Poor man."

I don't have the heart to tell this kind man that Walt will never visit the pawnshop again.

He picks up the painting, pulls the price tag from the back, and retrieves a small order pad to write down the five-digit code from the tag. When he reaches the price, he hesitates and looks up. "I tell you what, let's call it sixty."

The gesture catches me off guard and I almost yell out my status as a wealthy heiress. Fortunately, I realize his offer isn't intended to be offensive. He genuinely thinks I can't afford the painting and wants me to be able to give my grandmother a lovely present on her birthday. I am touched, and I simultaneously feel a little bit rotten.

"Thank you. I appreciate it."

He rings up the sale and I fish some cash out of my pocket. Luckily I have a lot of fives and ones, which reinforces the poor, young-girl angle of my con.

He takes the money and I lift the painting off the counter.

He reaches out a hand and grabs the frame.

For a moment, I worry that he's on to me and I'm tempted to yank the painting from his hand and run.

"It's still raining out, dear. Hold on a minute. I'll get a big trash bag and wrap it up real nice for you."

This guy is killing me. I'm going to have Silas anonymously send him money just as soon as I set up that philanthropic organization. Note to self: set up philanthropic fund thingy.

The owner returns with a black trash bag, slides the painting inside, rolls down the top, and tapes it shut tightly.

I thank him profusely, grab the painting, and escape before he can kill me with any additional kindness.

As soon as I get back to the car, I rip off the

trash bag. Why? I'll tell you why. Everyone knows that important stuff is frequently stashed behind family photos and—

Aha! One corner of the kraft paper backing is loose. Walt's visits to this painting were no sentimental journey.

I slip my hand carefully beneath the brown backing, feel around slowly, and—Yahtzee!

As I extract the single sheet of paper, I imagine all sorts of fantastical findings, including a possible treasure map. Instead, there are columns of numbers that have no relevance to my life.

Dates? No.

Phone numbers? No.

Addresses? I don't think so.

Safe deposit box numbers? How would I know?

Who cares? I bought a most likely stolen painting and discovered a hidden something or other. I'm going to go ahead and celebrate the crap out of that.

Let it be known that some, or all, of the posted speed limits may have been broken as I rush back to Pin Cherry Harbor. I burst into the apartment and am immediately underwhelmed by the lack of fanfare. "Grams? Grams? Where are you?"

No reply. I lean the painting up against the end of the four-poster bed and walk back into the bookstore. The Rare Books Loft is emptied of its studious bibliophiles, but two or three customers are still milling around on the first floor, so I can't go calling out for my Ghost-ma in the middle of the shop. Instead, I walk downstairs and find Twiggy in the back room. "Have you seen Grams?"

She turns slowly in her chair and gives me a look that can only be described as insufferable. "Now, how exactly would that happen, doll?"

"Right. Sorry, I keep forgetting I'm the only one who can see her. Well, except for Silas, but that's because of the glasses— Never mind. I'll keep looking."

As I walk out of the back room, Twiggy tosses a nugget of knowledge in my direction, "She always loved the top floor of the printing museum. Have you been up there?"

I shake my head. "Thanks. I'll check it out." I slip between the stacks and push open the metal door marked Employees Only.

The smell of ink, machinery, and history fills my nose. I run my hand over the gears and levers of the Gutenberg press. Someday, perhaps she'll tell me the story behind this collection, but today I have more urgent matters to discuss. I hurry up the staircase, trying to push away other memories clamoring to be acknowledged. "Grams? Grams? Are you in here?" I'm not sure why I'm whispering, but somehow being in the museum feels more like being in a library than being in the bookstore.

A sparkling ball of light floats toward me, and Grams materializes.

"That's the one you like, right?"

"Yes. That is the least alarming entrance." I smile warmly at the apparition. "What were you doing in here?"

Her face radiates with a light that actually makes me feel happier. "Come over here and see what I've been working on."

I follow her to a sturdy wooden workbench backed by hundreds of varied-sized cubbies. Beneath the bench are seven or eight thin drawers. One of them stands open, for display I assume.

Grams spins around and smiles at me. "Not for display. I opened it. I've been working on it for almost two weeks! And I finally got it open this far." She spins like a whirling dervish.

"You opened the drawer? I thought you couldn't move physical things. How did you—?"

"Who cares about that?" Grams' ghostly fingers point to a piece of parchment on the table. I lean over and see a quill pen resting on the blotter next to a sheet of parchment, bearing the phrase "I love you Mitzy" in a wriggly, scratchy hand that could be attributed to a child.

Tears spring to my eyes and salty drops make

blotches in the ink. "Shoot, sorry Grams. So sorry, I've ruined your note."

She hugs one arm around my shoulders and whispers, "You couldn't possibly ruin anything if you tried. I do love you, Mitzy."

"And I love you, Grams."

After basking in the familial love that's been missing from my life for a decade, I remember why I came looking for her in the first place. "I have to show you something, too. Come back to the apartment."

She chuckles, and her ghostly eyes twinkle. "I'll race ya." She disapparates and I rush down the stairs, charge through the bookshop, and thunder up the circular staircase. Foolishly thinking I can beat a ghost. As my hand reaches up to pull the candle handle, Grams' face pops through the sliding book-case door. "I win."

CHAPTER 18

FOLLOWING MY EARLY SUPPER at Myrtle's Diner, I saunter into the police station with every intention of telling Erick about the painting. Instead, I am bombarded with such a distracting flurry of activity I fear I'm in the wrong town. Even Furious Monkeys has managed to set down her phone.

Leaning over the counter, I nearly have to shout, "Sheriff Erick here?"

She jerks a thumb over her shoulder toward his office and I take that as permission.

Pushing past the swinging gate, I weave my way through the throng of unfamiliar faces and into Erick's office. Imagine my surprise when there's a gorgeous brunette in uniform sitting on the edge of his desk, joking with him in a much too familiar way.

"Ahem." I clear my throat loudly.

She turns and smiles warmly. Her crisp light-blue shirt is adorned with a colorful display of ribbons above her left breast pocket. "Good evening, ma'am. I'm Captain Truby of the US Coast Guard District 9." She extends her hand.

My hand shoots out reflexively and we exchange an awkward handshake. "Mitzy Moon, owner of the Bell, Book & Candle." I'm not sure why I added that, but it seems like titles are an important part of this trade.

She turns toward Erick and says, "I'll tell Junior you asked after him. He's a sergeant first class now. Anyway, I'll see if I can get the major crimes unit to cooperate. Read my report." She gestures to a document, printed in a remarkably neat hand, lying on his desk.

The same one Erick slipped into a folder on my previous visit.

She gives him a playful slug to the shoulder. "They argue about districts and control all day long. But the bottom line is if it happened out there on that lake, that's my jurisdiction. They can rattle their sabers all they want, but when it comes to the water, it's mine." She punches one fist into the other palm and marches out of Erick's office, giving me my first glimpse of my favorite law enforcement officer.

"Hey, Mitzy." He sighs and shakes his head.

Did he just use my first name? Holey moley! It's happening. My knees are wobbly and my stomach is flip-flopping. He just used my first name. I should talk now. I should say something nice to him. He looks exhausted, and stressed, and like he could use a shoulder massage. Don't say that. Dear Lord baby Jesus, don't say that. I go with, "What's all the ruckus out front?"

"It'll be all over the papers, so I might as well fill you in." He leans back in his chair and stretches his arms behind his head.

I am filled with anticipation, hoping that his shirt might come just a little untucked. No such luck. "What's going to be in the papers?" I ask.

"We traced that key—" He pauses and fixes me with an exasperated but warm stare. "A concerned citizen turned in a boat key which we traced back to Walter Johnson. The Coast Guard mounted a search for his boat. But it was the FBI divers who located the wreckage of Walt's boat first, and further investigation uncovered signs that a bomb had been placed aboard the vessel. They found evidence of a meth lab too, so it looks like Walt was cooking for Ivy. Whoever planted the device used the chemicals and a detonator to trigger the explosion. So it's definitely homicide, and possibly a lot of other things." He exhales and his hands fall firmly into his lap.

"What kinds of other things?"

He looks out the window of his office and scans across the frenzy of activity. "We've got members of something like six different law enforcement agencies out there trying to work as a joint task force while they fight over who gets credit. DEA. Tribal police. Coast Guard. Major Crimes. Homeland Security. FBI. And I'm sure I'm forgetting somebody."

"What about the *Men in Black?*"

He looks up at me and his blue-grey eyes fill with genuine concern. "The who?"

"You're not going to sit there and pretend like you never saw the movie *Men in Black,* are you?"

The creases vanish from his forehead and the worry in his eyes evaporates as a huge belly laugh grips him. Once he recovers, he looks up at me and smiles. "Thanks, Moon. I needed that."

I'm enraptured by the smile, but I mourn the loss of that momentary first-name-basis thing. Once again, I am Moon. "Anything else I can do?"

"Yeah, you can keep your nose out of this. Way out of this. Take one look out there and you'll see that I've got my hands full. I don't have time to babysit an amateur sleuth, poking around in dangerous business where she doesn't belong."

"I'm not sure if I should be insulted or flattered, Erick." I smile in what I hope is a seductive yet friendly manner.

"Take it however you want, Moon. Just back away from this, all right?" He stands and I get the distinct feeling that our banter is over.

I nod in the most noncommittal way possible and take the long way out of the station. If my meandering exit provides me with a nugget or two of information, what harm could that do?

My super snooping at the sheriff's station garners me some juicy tidbits. I mentally pat myself on the back as I hurry down the unseasonably sweltering sidewalk to the promise of air-conditioning at Myrtle's for my meeting with Diane.

As soon as I enter, there is something off about the energy in the diner. Yes, I know I just referred to the energy in the diner as though it's a real thing. I twist the ring on my left hand around and around my finger, afraid to look down and possibly experience another vision. Instead, I march to a booth and slide in, desperately struggling to ignore the tickling hairs on my forearms.

Odell gives me the customary wave through the orders-up window and Tally delivers my soda. "Are you enjoying the Indian summer, Mitzy?"

"Are we still allowed to say that?"

Tally looks at me as though a horn has sprouted between my eyes. "What else would we call it, dear?" She toddles over to offer refills to the patrons at the table in the front corner. While I sneak a peek at my ring.

It shifts from black to deepest blue and then to cold blue-grey. I don't want to admit how much it looks like the vast swath of water between here and the island. Something shimmers deeper within the image and I lean forward to get a better—

"Hi, are you Mitzy?"

I look up and know in an instant that this is Diane. She has her mother's cheekbones and the same shiny, straight black hair. "Yes. And you must be Diane. Have a seat. I'm so sorry about your dad." I blurt it all out too quickly. My heart is racing and my head pounds with anxiety. Part of me is embarrassed that she caught me staring into my ring, while most of me is just incredibly uncomfortable discussing the death of a parent.

She tosses her bulging backpack onto the seat and slips in beside it. "Thanks. It's been tough. My dad was all I had, you know?"

Boy did I. "Yeah, I get it."

Tally sidles up to the table and tilts her head at Diane in that "you poor thing, how sad for you" kind of way. It was a look I grew to hate in the years following my mother's death. No matter how sincere it was intended, it always felt false and patronizing.

"What can I get ya, Diane?"

Diane smiles with more kindness than I could ever have mustered less than a week after my own mother's death. "Thanks, Tally, I'd love a piece of pin cherry pie, with a big scoop of ice cream and extra whip."

"Coming right up."

Diane seems like a solid person. Maybe we have more in common than I assumed. But I can't shake the heavy feeling of dread. So I try to drive it away with relentless banter. "So, Odell says you're going to college down in some place called the Twin Cities. Do you like it?"

She nods. "Yeah, my campus is in Minneapolis. But the cities are so close together, I guess that's how they got their name." She shrugs. "I like it all right."

"What's your major?" I can't believe I just ask that stupid question. I feel like a giant movie cliché.

"I'm studying forestry."

And silence.

Boy, this girl is not giving me anything to work with. "Oh, interesting." I grab a jam packet and tap it back and forth between my fingers, completely out of conversation topics.

"Are you going to the community college?" she asks.

It almost seems like that question is meant to put me down. I raise my guard a little before I respond. "No, I'm Isadora Duncan's granddaughter. I own the bookshop and the museum." There, let little miss college student deal with the fact that I'm a business owner in this community.

Diane leans back and a strange glint flashes in her eye for a moment and quickly disappears. "Oh right, I forgot about your connection to the Duncans."

I have no idea what she means by that snarky comment, but I am liking Diane less and less. I decide to ask the question that is the Achilles' heel of every college student. "So what do you plan to do after you graduate?" I lean back and cross my arms smugly.

She doesn't miss a beat. "Oh, I plan to put my forestry degree to use developing Osprey Island. Of course, it will be an ecologically sound development plan." She presses her lips together in a fine line.

Tally arrives with Diane's pie and a plate of fries for me. I take a break from the *stimulating* conversation and happily munch on my fried pieces of perfection.

"Wow, you really like french fries," she muses.

"Yeah. I figure I might as well eat what I want while my metabolism is still racing."

She shrugs and daintily picks at her slice of pie. After two more bites, she sets down her fork and pushes it away.

Having firsthand knowledge of the deliciousness of the pie at Myrtle's Diner and the exquisite creaminess of the ice cream, I find her gesture personally offensive. I slide my empty plate to the end of the table and ask, "You gonna finish that?" Pointing to her pie.

She gives me a look similar to Tally's "horn in the middle of your forehead" expression, but shakes her head.

With a huge smile, I reach across and slide her pie within striking distance. The platter is clean in moments. However, despite my physical satisfaction, my energetic antennae are still tickling. "Are you close with your mom?"

The query has the desired effect and Diane is thrown off balance.

For a split second I feel something beyond dread; something cold and frightening. Darn it. I wish I had a better understanding of these powers.

She smiles. "Since you're new around here, you might not know the story. It's a little hard to talk about. My mom left right after I was born, and I haven't seen her since."

"Oh gosh, I'm sorry. I didn't know. I just thought since she was on the island on Tuesday, you might have run into her."

Diane's eyes darken and her jaw muscles flex as

she grinds her teeth together. "What makes you think my mother was on the island on Tuesday?"

A wiser person would've avoided answering the question. But that isn't my style. "Well, I ran into her at Walt's trailer, out there next to the charred remains of Walleye Lodge. I thought maybe she let you know she was coming to town. Maybe she's here for the funeral?" I offer this option with zero knowledge of any funeral plans.

"I have no idea." Diane unzips her backpack with far too much care and fishes around inside for a second.

I catch a glimpse of the contents, but look away before she notices.

When her hand reappears it contains a couple of crumpled bills that she sets on the table. "I've actually got to go to the mortuary right now. Like I said, if it was my mother that you saw, I had no idea she was in town." She launches out of the booth dragging her pack behind, and looks out the front door.

"So, it was nice meeting you, Diane."

"Sure. You too." She slings the bag over one shoulder and leaves without so much as a wave to her uncle Odell.

He looks through the window and shakes his head.

I add a few bills to the wadded up cash Diane

left on the table and I knock a coin loose while attempting to flatten the bills into one pile. I pick up the coin, which is about the size of a quarter, but it's definitely not a quarter. Imagine my surprise when I read the word "Canada" embossed on the face of the coin next to the image of a deer-thing, possibly an elk. It has large antlers and it kind of looks like the elk I've seen back in Arizona. I slip the coin in my pocket, wave to Odell, like a decent person, and walk back to the bookstore.

The scene that awaits me in the apartment could best be described as a silent movie. Silas has on his special glasses that allow him to see the ghost of grandmothers past, and Grams is doing her best Marcel Marceau pantomime in an attempt to communicate with the aged barrister—who can only see, but not hear her.

She sees me and sighs with relief. "Oh thank heavens! I was absolutely running out of ideas. Now you can translate, Mitzy."

"Hello, Silas."

"Good afternoon, Miss Moon."

"Oh please, Sheriff Erick is bad enough. I don't need two people in this town calling me Miss Moon."

Silas chuckles and his magicked glasses make his eyes appear twice as large as normal.

"Mitzy, you need to stop spinning that ring

around your finger and tell Silas what's going on," chides Grams.

When she's right she's right. I take a seat in the scalloped-back chair and interlace my fingers to keep them from shaking. "Silas?"

"Yes, Mitzy."

"Grams wants me to tell you something."

He nods and his jowls wiggle waggle.

"She thinks I need to learn more about my gift."

"The gift may be hereditary." He looks up at Grams and they both nod in agreement. "What kinds of things have you been feeling?"

"It mainly seems to happen when I wear the ring." I show him the circa 1970s mood ring. "I felt some emotions that came from Grams and I felt some other strange things. The weirdest was today at the diner. I felt this odd sense of dread. And then I met Diane, and—"

Silas puts up his hand, gesturing me for me to stop. "Did you feel the dread before you met Diane or *as* you met Diane?"

Closing my eyes to shut out any distractions, I replay the events at the diner. "I definitely felt the dread before she came in. But I also felt something uncomfortable after she arrived. She's not that nice a person." I look over at Grams. "I'm actually kind of surprised you paid for her college. Something isn't quite right about her. And she said she was going to use her forestry degree to develop Osprey Island. She gave me some nonsense about how it was an ecological development plan, but I kind of wonder how the Tribal Council is going to feel about that."

Silas strokes his thumb and forefinger over his bushy mustache and Grams swirls around the room like a maniacal ghost merry-go-round.

"Oh, and there was this." I reach into my pocket with my left hand and fish out the Canadian coin, but as soon as it touches the band of my ring, images flood through my head. Diane on a plane. Diane's passport. Duffle bags. Plastic wrapping. Diane driving a car. Duffle bags, but no clothes.

I drop the coin on the floor, stand, and step away from it as though it's a rattlesnake.

"Tell me exactly what happened, Mitzy." The calm voice of Silas utters a single command.

I describe events as best I can with my limited vocabulary of these strange occurrences and I explain the images that I saw.

Silas stands and stares through his glasses at my grandmother's ghost. "Isadora, she may possess more than one gift."

My grandmother rushes toward me and wraps her phantom arms around me.

Awkwardly, I attempt to return the embrace. I can feel the tingling of her energy against my body and I feel safe and loved. But I have no idea what is going on. "What is he talking about, Grams?"

"Well, as I told you, dear. I only ever got visions. Some people call them premonitions. But if Silas is right, and you can feel things and see things, then you may have more than one gift." She smiles like a proud mama.

A chill races across my skin and I place a hand over my mouth to stifle a gasp. "What does it mean if I heard something?"

Silas takes off his magic spectacles and walks toward me, emanating a strange and commanding power. "Elaborate."

"Earlier today, downstairs in the stacks. Pyewacket was terrorizing this guy, who I'm pretty sure is named Gary. And when Gary walked toward me, I heard the word 'danger'."

Silas cleans the glasses meticulously and slips the curved metal arms over his ears. "Do you know what this means?"

I shake my head nervously.

"I believe you are a true psychic, Mitzy. You receive messages audibly, visually, through sensations, and even sometimes through a sense of knowing that cannot be explained. These are valuable gifts. But you must learn to decipher the messages, or you will waste countless hours running in circles pursuing phantom wisps of ideas that you can never

comprehend. The true gift of a psychic is not in re-
ceiving the information, it's in properly translating
the tidings."

Despite every effort to nod my head, no part of
my body will move. Somehow this sad little orphan
is suddenly special beyond measure. First a family,
and now I have some incomprehensible gift or
maybe gifts? It's all way too much.

Grams is shamelessly listening to my thoughts
and sobbing uncontrollably. I'm sure they're happy
tears. But all I can think is how much I wish my
powers could give her a ghostly handkerchief. I look
up at her and we share a tearful chuckle.

"Let's begin with the images from the coin."

Good ol' Silas. Always the voice of reason.

CHAPTER 19

AFTER MY CRASH COURSE in Psychic Powers 101, I decide to give myself a pop quiz. I drive down to the train depot office and the docks. It seems like a good time to get a little more information from Gary about where he got his gun, and why.

The truth of the matter is I have no real context for the strange message, "Danger," that I heard when I bumped into Gary in the bookshop, but I also don't believe his visit was as innocent as he proclaimed. I park my car in the train depot parking lot. A car stops in the road to let me cross as I walk the block and a half to Final Destination, the dive bar where I first met Gary. I'm feeling so small-town that I almost wave, but I can't actually see the driver through the tinted windows. I pick up my pace and ignore the uneasy feeling in my chest.

As I enter this cubic zirconia in the rough, the scent of decades-old cigarette smoke, beer-stained carpet, and cheap cologne assaults my senses. And I mean just the regular five, not my supernatural ones. Gary is bent over the pool table in the back and I'm not proud to say that I instantly recognize him by his best feature.

I approach the table and lay a quarter on the bumper.

"I got this table all night," he says without looking up. His pool stick slides along the bridge he creates with his finger and smacks into the cue ball, which sends one of the solids rocketing into the corner pocket.

"Nice shot. You come here often?"

He stands with a quick jerk, smiles, and lays down his pool cue. "Well, what have we here?"

It's painfully obvious that he has not yet had the pleasure of recalling my name. "Moon, Mitzy Moon." I give him a wink.

His face pales in the dim light of the Pabst blue ribbon fixture slung low over the peeling green felt.

Not the best or worst reaction I've received since arriving in Pin Cherry Harbor. "Did you ever find your *phone?*" I emphasize "phone" in a way that I hope helps him understand that I in no way mean phone.

He leans back, tilts his head, and narrows his gaze. "Did you find something in your apartment?"

"Maybe." I prefer to keep it noncommittal until he admits what he actually lost. "What kind of phone did you lose?"

His fists ball up at his sides and he grumbles in a low and threatening tone, "The dangerous kind."

I raise my eyebrows and nod. "I did find something dangerous. However, since I'm so new in town, I thought it would be best to let the sheriff handle it."

Gary's expression flips from shocked to furious in the blink of an eye. He grips the bumper of the pool table and his knuckles shift to white as he growls, "That better be a joke."

I shake my head. "What do you need such a dangerous phone for in a safe little town like Pin Cherry?"

"You better mind your own business. And hope that nothing comes back on you."

I narrow my gaze. "Don't threaten me, Gary."

Gary's hand dives into his pocket. He pulls up his phone and taps at the screen. "Don't go anywhere. I gotta make a quick call." He steps outside.

Taking the liberty of collecting all the pool balls, I rack them and start a new game with a fresh break. I happen to knock in a solid and a striped, so I'm sizing up my best shot when the door opens behind me. I choose to play it coy and pretend to be too involved in my game to acknowledge Gary's return.

Footsteps approach.

As I feel a surge of anger that does not belong to me rising in my chest, I hesitate a moment too long.

Some kind of damp, musty smelling cloth bag is pulled over my head and a strong arm encircles my neck. I kick, scratch, and attempt to yell for help. But despite my lungs screaming for oxygen, I can't breathe.

My eyes open and after several minutes, I can make out thin cracks of light above me. I'd like to move my hands, but they're securely tied in front of me. I lean slowly to the left and feel cold metal beneath me. That is when I notice the movement. No matter how still I remain, I still feel bobbing and swaying.

I'm on a boat. And not the fun party-song kind with T-Pain.

I'm in the bottom of a gasoline-smelling boat on the lake.

With no idea how long I was unconscious, I could be a mere one hundred yards from the bar, or I could be out in the middle of one of the five largest freshwater lakes in the world.

Panic grips my heart. My breathing races and I can hear my heart beating like a drum in my ear.

No one knows where I am.

I didn't tell anyone where I was going.

I didn't leave a note.

I could suffocate.

Calm yourself, Mitzy. You can see daylight, and that means you can breathe. Stay calm and use what you've got.

What I've got is nothing. I'm stashed in some boat, on some lake, with no food or water.

Explore the whole space. You might be surprised by what you find.

I don't know where this calm voice is coming from, but it's driving me insane. Apparently, there is a perfectly serene half of my brain that isn't at all rattled by my sudden kidnapping.

I twist to get my feet under me and that's when I discover there's also a rope securely knotted around my ankles.

I scoot along the floor like a seal out of water and see what I can find. There's something that feels like a lifejacket. Then a small metal case. I try the latch and it pops open. Inside I feel around and can identify Band-Aids, packets of what must be antibacterial ointment—basic first-aid stuff.

Basic first-aid stuff might include scissors!

I meticulously search every inch of the metal case.

Aha! Scissors.

I grab those and slip them into the front pocket of my jeans for later use.

Continuing my search, I find something that feels like a boat cushion, some empty plastic bags, several large canvas duffle bags filled with tightly wrapped bundles covered in thick plastic, secured with tape.

Finally, pushed up against the metal hull, two cases of plastic bottles. I stretch the wrap secured around the bottles, with my teeth and tied hands, until it tears and wiggle one loose. I twist off the cap and sniff at the contents. Smells like nothing more than bottled water.

What if it's laced with something?

Unless it's laced with strychnine, how much worse could your situation get?

I have to agree with Tranquil Mitzy. I decide to take a small sip and wait an arbitrary amount of time to see what happens.

I take my sip and secure the lid.

I scoot back to my original location, set the bottle next to me, extract the scissors, and begin the process of snipping my way to freedom with the equivalent of child's safety scissors.

Having no way to calculate the passing of time,

I judge halfway through one loop of the rope encircling my wrists to be enough time to deem the liquid in the bottle safe.

I take two more sips and replace the cap.

After I make it all the way through one loop of rope, the boat rocks suddenly and loud voices on deck drift through the cracks.

There's no time to cut through the remaining rope. I twist and pull my wrists and yank my hands free as fast as I can, but my race against time is for nothing. Whoever boarded has no interest in the cargo. They go straight to the main cabin and fire up the engines.

This new purposeful movement could be bringing me closer to home or taking me irretrievably farther from rescue.

The worse news is that the aroma of fuel intensifies. A wave of nausea turns my skin cold and clammy.

My hands are now free and I untie my ankles as well, but to what end. I lean back against the curved hull, close my eyes, and for some reason think of Pyewacket.

Crazy, brilliant, irritating feline. He serves no purpose but to annoy me on a daily basis. However, the thought of never seeing him again breaks my heart.

Robin Pyewacket Goodfellow, if I should never

see you again, I would like to say, I think I love you. It's an unfamiliar emotion, and it might be considered transference or objectification. But you've done more for me during our short acquaintance than any humans I can think of in my twenty-one years on this planet.

If I'd had the chance to grow old with you, Pye, I would've considered myself lucky. However, it seems my impulsive snooping is what finally did me in. I sit here in the hull of some mysterious vessel, motoring across some enormous body of water, to some unknown destination. No matter what happens, I'm glad I had the chance to be your friend.

P.S. Don't blame Gary. It's probably not his fault. I actually never saw who put the bag over my head.

I'm not sure why I am so anxious to clear Gary's name at this point. Something about the smell of the man who grabbed me didn't register as Gary. What am I actually doing right now? Am I "clairodorant?" If I were examining the evidence, I'd say he was the most likely suspect.

For all I know, that call he received might've instructed him to nab me.

I should've been paying attention, counting the minutes, or listening for sounds. There will be no way for me to re-create the trajectory that my kidnappers took and lead the police to the stash.

Of course, since there's no chance of being rescued, details hardly seem important.

The engine cuts off and the voices on deck resume. As I strain my senses, I may even hear voices coming from farther away, possibly the shore or the dock.

Metal grates against the rough surface and clunks over my head. There's a splash followed by the whizzing sound of a rope sliding over the side of the boat. I don't know a ton about maritime happenings, but I'd say we just dropped anchor.

There's a steady rhythmic splashing and a soft thunk as something bumps the side of the boat.

My first instinct is *Jaws*; my second is a small craft.

Something metal slaps against the side of the boat and one, wait no, two people climb down what must be a chain ladder and hop into the smaller craft. They shove off and the rhythmic paddling grows faint.

I wait several minutes, unsure of my next move.

If there's no one else on the boat, this is as close as you're going to get to shore. Whatever shore it is. Now's your chance.

My chance to what?

Swim for it.

What? I can't believe what I'm hearing. Or

what I'm telling myself. Everything is jumbled in my head.

Get off this boat.

All right. All right. Geez! Other Mitzy is getting pushy. I take a deep breath, twist the ring on my finger and try to feel for other people who might still be on board.

Still unclear as to how my gifts work, or how to interpret the messages, the best I can do is get myself out of this hold and hope no one is standing guard.

I take a piece of the rope, tie a knot around the water bottle, and tie the other around my waist. I have no idea where I'm going, but I grew up in the desert. Water is life.

I creep toward the dimming slivers of light and push against the hatch. It does not budge.

I'm locked in. Of course I would be locked in. When you have valuable cargo, you don't just leave it sitting out in the open.

Valuable cargo? Assuming that's not me, what else is down here?

I feel my way back past the lifejackets and the first-aid kit to the tightly wrapped plastic bundles. Attempting to rip through the plastic with my fingers is unsuccessful, so I retrieve the scissors and slice one open. The resulting spillage sounds like the tiny beads in a Native American rain stick.

I tip the package to staunch the flow and reach in with my fingers. Small round bits with smooth edges—pills! Oh, *Mighty Aphrodite,* they're pills.

Drugs!

Somehow, I know in my gut that I'm on the smuggler's boat. But before I can plan my next move, my eyes are drawn to the mood ring . . .

And clear as day I see an image of Diane's backpack. When she unzipped it in the diner to dig out her cash, there was something in the bag. Something plastic. I only saw a corner of whatever was bundled into her bag, but if I can get one of these to shore and—

Now is your only chance.

The calm voice in my head makes perfect sense. It's now or never.

I grab a life jacket, tie the webbing strap around one of the un-opened plastic-wrapped bundles, and slide back toward the hatch.

This time I take a methodical approach and feel around the edges for hinges or hopefully . . . Bingo! A handle.

I give the handle a cautious twist, but the metal on metal screech is loud enough to wake the dead.

My throat tightens and I freeze in horror.

I don't know how long to wait. Two minutes? An hour?

No footsteps. No voices.

I push upward and the hatch squeaks open.

I shove the lifejacket and bundle of pills through first. Then I wait.

No gunshots. No running footsteps.

Risking a peek, I push my head through the opening. The sun has slipped out of sight and the whistling of a crisp twilight wind is gaining strength.

I slither out of the hold and crawl across the deck toward the edge. I peep over the side and see nothing but blue-black water as far as the eye can see. It's only a matter of time before the boat swivels on the anchor and this side faces the shore.

Arizona may not have ten thousand lakes, but I did take a couple of trips up to Lake Powell. And I happen to know that when you jump off the deck of a boat into the water, it makes a large, loud splash.

I need that ladder.

Crawling across the deck to the other side of the boat, the top of the chain ladder hooks through two metal loops before it disappears over the side. I glimpse over and see the shore, but the wind is pushing the boat away from land in a wide arc. I might have a minute at the most to climb down the ladder unseen.

Waiting until the breeze swings this side of the boat out of sight of shore, I crouch below the rail.

It's now or never. "Never" brings fresh spikes of fear to my skin.

I slip my arm through the lifejacket and throw my legs over the side. My foot slips on the metal step and my left leg pushes through the ladder, catching me in a most uncomfortable position. I stifle a scream, untangle my water bottle and rope from the ladder, readjust my limbs, and start down a second time.

The wind has picked up. My side of the boat whirls back toward danger. The water is just below me. If I jump there'll be a small splash. If I wait . . .

I jump. The splash is not enormous, but it's also not unnoticeable. I hope whoever has watch— wasn't. I hold the lifejacket in front of me and kick my feet under the water as hard as I can.

No more splashing. No more sounds. I'm slipping through the water like a—

Oh, dear Lord baby Jesus, what is in this lake? Are there such things as freshwater sharks? Do beavers eat people?

I kick my legs faster and my quads burn. Daylight is gone and the dim afterglow is slipping away.

I'm still fifty yards from shore. The muscles in my legs are going to explode before I ever make it to land.

Something bumps into me and a squeak escapes my mouth.

I duck my head under water to hide my con-spicuous white hair. When I pop up, shouts from the beach shatter the hushed air.

Kicking as though my life depends on it, and let's be honest it does, I race toward shore. Some-thing else bumps me, but this time the hard impact on my hipbone confirms it's a rock.

Land! I get my feet under me and stumble my way to dry land. I unhook the lifejacket and drag it up into the trees, out of sight.

I'd love to stay here until morning so that I have more light to find my way, but by morning I'm sure to be discovered.

With the plastic-wrapped bundle of contraband under my right arm, I move through the trees slowly but steadily. I can feel the ground stretching up-ward before me.

By the time I risk a backward glance, the smug-gler's fire on the beach looks far below. I must be near the bluff where Nimkii, my dad, and I first spied Ivy Lapointe.

Pushing past the row of large granite boulders, I soon feel the familiar stinging of the thorns on the raspberry vines as they tear at my skin. I've honestly never been so pleased to be in so much pain.

I continue forward, following a sense of direc-tion that is not my own. Exhaustion tugs at my mus-cles, and despite my desire for the safety of human contact, I'm forced to crawl into the deep under-brush before I collapse.

Multicolored sunlight filtering through the trees coaxes me awake.

For a split second, I smile and stretch my arms. But then the intense pain in my legs and the abject fear in my heart heighten all my senses.

There are voices. Multiple voices in the forest.

Part of me wants to call out and be found; the other part realizes the inherent danger in mistaking enemy for friend.

Creeping farther into the thick ferns, I wait in silence.

I could swear they're calling my name. However, that's little consolation. It wouldn't be that hard for the kidnappers to obtain my name. I did introduce myself to Gary right before I got nabbed. I continue to wait.

Rhythmic vibration trembles the ground beneath me. Those aren't footsteps. That's a horse!

The smugglers do not have horses. That must be Nimkii. It has to be.

Struggling with my decision, I hesitate, unable to make a choice. Luckily the loud and somewhat worried voice of my father makes the decision for me. "Mitzy? Mitzy, it's all right. It's Dad."

I crawl out onto the trail. My throat is too clogged with emotion to call for help.

Thundering hooves clamor to a halt nearby. The solid thud of my father's feet hitting the dirt and his strong arms scooping me up is one of the top five moments of my life. Guaranteed.

"I've got her!" he calls. Other voices and shouts blur as the safety envelops me and I struggle to hang on to consciousness.

Truly believing nothing could improve on this moment, I've never been so happy to be wrong.

An angelic light seems to surround Erick as he jogs down the trail toward my dad and me. The look of concern and relief on his face threatens to break my heart.

"We need to get her to the hospital, Jacob." Erick grabs his radio and directs the police boat to stand by at the dock below Chez Osprey. Then his strong hand reaches for my leg with unexpected tenderness. He carefully slides up my pant leg and mumbles, "There's quite a bit of blood."

At first, I can't imagine where the blood came from, but unwelcome memories of the thorny raspberry vines worm their way to the surface. However, that pain is instantly pushed away by a more urgent memory. "Pills," I whisper, and weakly gesture toward the underbrush beside the trail.

Erick removes his hand from my leg, nods, and

prowls into the scrub. After several minutes he surfaces with the tightly wrapped plastic package, which I stole from the cargo hold. He looks at me and tilts his head in the most endearing way. "This looks like a standard bundle of counterfeit opioids. Probably has a street value of about $3,000, give or take. The smugglers trade this stuff for meth. No money to launder . . ." He shakes his head and sighs. "I'm not even going to ask, Moon. I'll take your statement once the doctor patches you up."

Jacob walks toward his horse.

"Wait," I manage to whisper.

My dad stops. "Sheriff, she's got more to say."

Erick hurries over. "I can handle the rest, Moon. I am the sheriff, in case you've forgotten."

His words are gruff, but his gentle blue eyes are brimming with tenderness. My information is crucial, so I force my exhausted brain to focus. "Diane —" I cough and my arm is too sore to make any effort to cover my mouth. "Diane had a bundle like that one. Pills. In her backpack."

"All right, Moon. We'll check it out. She's staying at the hotel by the Coast Guard station." He pats my dad on the shoulder and adds, "Get her to the hospital, Jacob. I'm sure Deputy Paulsen would love to pick up Diane. I'd ask Truby, but she's sweeping the far side of the island to see if they can intercept the smugglers."

With that, my dad jogs toward his horse, carrying me like I'm nothing more than a sack of groceries. He gingerly places me on Cranberry's back and swings up onto the horse's haunches, behind the saddle, as he kicks us into motion.

The ride back to Chez Osprey is longer than I remember and far more uncomfortable. Every aching muscle, bruise, and scratch throbs with pain. I don't have a clear memory of being transported from horse to boat, but at some point I wake up in the hospital. Woozy from whatever medication is dripping through my IV, I scan the room almost expecting to see Grams floating next to my dad.

No such luck.

However, I'm pleased to see the room contains my three favorite guys. My dad, my lawyer, and my secret crush.

Jacob leans forward and squeezes my hand. "I've got quite a lot to tell you, sweetheart. But the sheriff needs to get your statement. My news can wait."

Erick approaches the foot of the bed and smiles, in what I prefer to believe is more than a professional way. "Miss Moon, are you strong enough to give me your statement?"

Consenting with a careful tilt of my head, I hold up a hand. "I need a sip of water first."

My father grabs the dusty-rose-colored plastic

container from my bedside table and turns the straw toward me. As I take a long sip, he offers up some commentary. "That was smart of you to tie that water bottle to your waist." His voice cracks a little and his eyes are misty. Another thing I seem to have in common with my father, offering practical advice or compliments rather than expressing deep emotion.

Sheriff Erick retrieves his notepad and clicks his pen. "I'm ready when you are, Moon."

"Did you get Diane?"

Erick's hands drop to his sides in surrender. "If it will move this interview along . . . Paulsen brought Diane in yesterday. The girl still had the pills on her, but swore that she was trying to return them. She wouldn't say if they came from Ivy, but the packaging was identical to the bundle you found on the smuggler's boat." He exchanges a defeated look with Silas. "That was all we got out of her before she asked for a lawyer."

I roll my head to the left. "You?"

Silas harrumphs into his bushy mustache. "Isadora would've wanted it."

I can't help but wonder if his use of the past tense is for Erick's sake. I know how persuasive Grams can be, even with only the power of pantomime. I raise an eyebrow.

"We are discussing options with the district attorney." Silas smooths his whiskers and looks away.

Erick raises his pen and pad a second time. "How 'bout that statement, Moon?"

I relay the story of being grabbed from the Final Destination, but I leave out anything remotely related to the terror that I felt. I explain how I escaped from the boat, swam ashore, and came to be discovered on the trail by my father.

"Is there anything else you remember, Miss Moon?"

As I open my mouth to say no, a snippet of conversation pops into my head. The voices on deck had been shouting about something. I close my eyes and force my unwilling brain to replay those terrifying hours trapped in the dark, damp hold.

"Did she fall asleep?" asks Erick.

Silas clears his throat and replies, "I believe she is attempting to access the memory."

Leave it to Silas to make it sound so complicated. As I drift deeper into the recollection, I hear the phrase, ". . . the drop on Saturday. We get rid of the girl on the way. Ivy said tie her up and throw her overboard, and let the lake do the rest." I shiver involuntarily as the words reveal how close I came to death. My eyes pop open and I blink several times to push the emotion back down.

"Did you remember something?" Erick's pen is poised above his pad.

"They said something about a drop this Saturday." I choose to leave out the bit about how they planned to dump my body. My dad looks like he's holding it together by a thread as it is.

"Did they say where the drop was?" Erick raises a hopeful eyebrow.

I shake my head.

"That's okay. If you think of anything else, you give me a call. All right?"

"All right."

Erick walks out of my room and stops to give instructions to the deputy guarding my door. Poor Deputy Paulsen. Of all the things she would like to be doing, protecting me has to be at the absolute bottom of her list.

Silas walks over and nudges the door closed.

My father leans in and squeezes my hand with renewed force. "Don't ever pull a stunt like that again. You hear me?"

I'm certain I didn't pull this stunt on purpose. I'd like to defend myself, but twenty-twenty hindsight has clearly shown me that venturing into a seedy dive bar without so much as leaving a note wasn't my best-laid plan.

"I suggest you share your news, Jacob," prompts Silas.

My father nods. "Right. I've decided to hang onto the railroad business. Cal left it to me in the will and I could sell it for a pretty penny, but I don't need the cash. Keeping it in the family seems like the right way to honor his memory and thank him for having enough faith in me to change his will. But the real news is that when I was going over the books, I found some things that didn't add up. I wouldn't have thought much of it, but those discrepancies along with what happened to you . . . I'm not sure how much to share with the sheriff."

There's definitely something Jacob is leaving out of his story, but at the moment the biggest question on my mind is how did everyone know where to look for me? "How did you find me?"

Silas chuckles and Jacob shrugs before he replies. "I guess we have to give Pyewacket most of the credit." He looks at Silas, and the lawyer shakes his jowls affirmatively.

"Pyewacket? That cat can't even find his own Fruity Puffs. I can't imagine how he helped in a missing-persons case." I want to chuckle but my tender throat rebels and delivers a fit of coughing instead.

My dad offers me water as he launches into the story. "When you didn't turn up for breakfast at the diner, I went to the apartment. As soon as I

opened the bookcase door, Pyewacket started running circles around the room like he was
possessed."

I attempt to lift my hands in a "who cares" gesture but the muscles in my arms are too exhausted
from my lengthy swim to respond. So I mumble,
"He is possessed."

Jacob's eyes widen as he adds, "No argument
here." He eagerly continues, "He pulled a pair of
chewed up shoes out of the trash can, spilled a glass
of water from the bedside table, and knocked a
photo album off the bookcase. All in the space of
about sixty seconds. I had no idea what he was
trying to tell me, so I rang Silas."

Silas bobs his head several times before picking
up the story. "Pyewacket has always shown a curious affection for the unseen. I took the various
clues he provided and made a list of their potential
meanings. Eventually I came to understand that the
boat shoes, the water, and the photo album con-
taining pictures of Chez Osprey, Walleye Lodge
and Tavern, and, of course, Ivy Lapointe, could
only mean one thing."

My father jumps in with the solution. "We suspected you were in a boat on the water, somehow
connected to Ivy. When the general manager down
at the depot reported your car in the parking lot, I
made the connection to the bar." He looks at Silas,

back to me and shrugs. "I'm not proud to say I roughed up Gary pretty bad."

"Is he the one who grabbed me?"

"Sounds like he was a middleman. Ivy had something on him and delivering you was going to make 'em square."

"That slime ball didn't even know my name. If I hadn't introduced myself, none of this would've happened."

"I wouldn't be so sure. According to the story I . . . dragged out of him, Ivy texted him a picture of you after we met her on the island. It was just small-town bad luck that he'd already . . ." My father blushes and clearly doesn't know how to refer to my one-night-stand with Gary.

I jump in and rescue him. "We'd already met." I nod for him to continue.

"Yes. So he was just following orders." Jacob's jaw clenches and his gaze hardens.

A fresh set of horrifying chills slithers down my spine. "Wait, that was before I even knew Ivy was involved."

Jacob looks down at the floor. "When I introduced you as my daughter, she saw an heiress and an opportunity. She was planning on asking for a two-million-dollar ransom."

Too shocked to respond, I can't help but wonder if I'm worth two million.

As though he reads my mind, Jacob mumbles, "I would've paid whatever they asked to keep you safe, Mitzy."

My throat tightens with emotion. "Let's hope you never have to."

My father tries to turn my frown upside down. "I guess it's a good thing that gun fell under the bed before he had a chance to use it."

I would have to agree. And I would also have to nominate Pyewacket as feline most likely to have knocked it under the bed. It seems that cat not only has his own set of multiple lives, but he's appointed himself my personal guardian caracal.

"So if there's going to be a drop on Saturday . . . What day is it?" I ask.

"Today is Saturday." Silas strokes his bushy grey mustache.

I fight through the pain and force myself into a sitting position. "I need to get out of here. If I can get my hands on that packet of pills, I might be able to figure out more information about the drop."

My father rises to his full six feet and change and places a firm hand on my shoulder. "You've done more than enough for our local law enforcement. They'll take it from here."

My mind is racing. I look down at my left hand and see the ring is gone. "My ring!"

"I've kept it safe for you, Mitzy." Silas fishes

around in the breast pocket of his brown tweed suit coat, retrieves the ring, takes an unhurried stance, and places it in my hand.

I slip it on my finger and wait. I recall the image of the pills tumbling through my fingers in the hull of the boat. There were also large duffle bags of some kind. At least ten? It was so dark I can't be sure. I focus on the image of the tumbling pills and stare into the ring.

Nothing.

Silas puts a hand on my arm and whispers, "Clear your mind. Don't force information into the vision, simply let it unfold."

I breathe in and out, trying to push the images of boats, pills, icy water—all of it—out of my mind. I look back at the ring and see greenish-gold swirls. For a moment those stupid boat shoes appear and I nearly lose my focus. I exhale and push that image away. It is quickly replaced by a photo of my late grandpa Cal Duncan holding up a moose's head by the antlers. I remember this photo from his office at the train depot, and the man next to him . . . Nimkii!

My eyes pop open. My throat goes dry.

Jacob leans toward me. "What? What is it?"

"A photo from the wall in grandpa Cal's office at the train depot. The hunting photo, with the moose and Nimkii."

Jacob looks at Silas. "Do you think he's involved with Ivy?"

Silas smooths his mustache twice before answering. "We'll have time to unbraid that wreath at a later date. But I am certain the vision of the train depot is no coincidence."

My father's face lights up and he nods enthusiastically. "The discrepancies in the cargo manifests. This could be the connection. I'll let the sheriff know." He steps into the hall to pass his information on to Deputy Paulsen.

Silas squeezes my hand. "You're getting better, Mitzy. Each time you practice using your gifts, they will improve."

"Can you get me out of here?"

"I will not be party to you taking any further risks." Silas harrumphs and crosses his arms.

"I'm just anxious to see Grams."

The barrister's stern expression softens and he nods. "I'll see what I can do."

Hiding behind a pleasant smile, I silently plot— and once I'm out of here, I'll see what I can do.

CHAPTER 20

BEFORE I CAN PUT a second foot onto the floor inside the bookshop, Grams is all over me.

"Don't you ever scare me like that again, young lady. Do you hear me?"

Making a conscious effort to peer around the stacks, I make sure it's all clear before answering. "Yes, Grams. I've already received sufficient lectures from Jacob, Silas, and Erick."

"Well I don't give a rat's behind! You can hear another one from me. The very idea! Wandering into that shady establishment, without so much as a word to me." She crosses her bejeweled limbs over her vintage gown and scowls.

At times like these, I have to admit I'm grateful she's not a vengeful spirit.

"You are going to experience some vengeance if you pull a stunt like that again."

I point to my lips and shake my head. She knows the rules about reading my thoughts.

She stares at me, and I worry there might be flames flickering in her ghostly eyes. Before I can negotiate a truce—

Pyewacket leaps off the stairs and literally bowls me over. His rough tongue must be removing a layer of skin from my face, yet I can't bring myself to push him off. He's the reason they knew where to look. I scratch him roughly between the tufted ears and eventually roll out from underneath his affectionate assault.

I rush up the circular staircase into the apartment. The painting lies untouched on my coffee table. I slide my fingers under the paper backing and extract the piece of paper for the second time.

"What is this? It has to be important. No one hides a piece of paper in the back of a painting just for grins and giggles."

Grams is still sulking and refuses to respond.

Holding the sheet, I pace the length of the apartment as I stare at the random columns of numbers. Not dates, or phone numbers, or addresses, or—

"Geocaching!" I shout to the four walls.

Despite her anger, Grams materializes. "What are you going on about?"

"I finally figured out what these columns of numbers mean. It's a list of latitudes and longitudes that directs you to a physical location where something has been hidden. It's called geocaching. It's all the rage with my generation. Don't get me started. But this might be how Walt was planning to cut Ivy out of the exchanges. He knew he could make a lot more money without a middleman. He could've been carefully building up his supply of meth while he ferreted out Ivy's Canadian contact."

"That does make sense. Especially if he found out about what Ivy was doing to Diane."

"What do you mean? How do you know what Ivy was doing to Diane?"

"I know you only met the girl the one time, but I've known the child her whole life. She's a good girl who loves her father, and never wanted anything to do with her mother."

This information doesn't fit with my impression of Diane in the diner, but Silas did tell me that interpreting the messages is the most important part. The feeling of dread could have been related to Diane's regret, or fear of someone discovering she was in possession of the pills. Maybe? It's all so confusing. "If Diane was meeting with Ivy on Walt's behalf, why?"

"I don't know the whole story, dear, but Silas came by and asked if I'd have a problem with him representing the girl. She told him she had enough information to make a deal."

"What information?" I pace toward the four-poster bed.

"She wouldn't tell Silas until they gave her a mutiny."

Turning slowly, I squint at the apparition. "A mutiny?" Laughter grips me and my aching muscles protest each guffaw. "I'm pretty sure you mean immunity, Grams."

"Oh yes, that makes much more sense. I was so flustered about you disappearing, I wasn't thinking straight."

"Ree-ow." Proud with a hint of humility.

Stooping to scratch his insufferable belly, I reply, "Yes, Pye, it is fortunate that you were thinking straight."

Grams descends to coddle the daylights out of the large fur baby while I make another lap around the apartment and stare at the list of numbers.

If I'm correct about these numbers indicating geocaches of methamphetamine, there must be fifteen secret stashes. No matter how fast Walt was cooking, I doubt he could stash this much and keep up with Ivy's orders. Maybe she didn't burn down the Walleye Inn. Maybe Walt burned it down himself!

I spin around and look at Grams. "Maybe Walt burned down the Walleye to throw Ivy off his trail. Maybe he convinced her that his lab blew up. That's a thing, right? Meth labs blow up all the time. Don't they?"

Grams nods encouragingly. "I've no idea, sweetheart. That's more of a 'your generation' thing, but I'm sure they do. That seems to be the only option that makes sense, because you said he sold off all his valuables in an estate sale before the fire."

"Exactly. So he knew there was going to be a fire, but I don't think Ivy knew about the estate sale."

Grams asks, "What about the business card?"

"The business card for Gershon Antiquities that Erick found near Boilerplate Beach wasn't wet or burned, so it couldn't have washed ashore with Walt. Someone saw that body before Pyewacket and I discovered it. If that someone was working for Ivy—" A shudder chills my skin as I wonder what may have happened to Mr. Gershon. "What if Ivy figured out the plan? What if she suspected Walt of double-crossing her and sent someone to shake Lars down for information?"

"Do you think that's how Lars ended up dead?"

"No idea. But Walt was keeping this painting at

the pawnshop for a reason. If Lars had known about this list"—I wave the sheet of coordinates—"I'm sure he would've handed it over without a fight."

"That poor man." Grams sniffles. "He died for nothing."

I grab my phone and type in the first set of numbers from the secret list. It appears to be in the middle of the lake. "How am I going to check this out? I definitely can't involve Dad." As I stare at the blinking dot on my phone, a lovely plan unfolds. "It's just a boat ride. No one will even know where I've gone."

"Mizithra Achelois Moon! You will not go hunting down these dangerous drug caches on your own!"

I lay the piece of paper down, take a picture, upload it to the cloud, and slip the paper under the lining on the back of the framed painting.

All the way down the circular staircase and to the heavy metal side door, she's lecturing me about the folly of youth.

Grams stops right below the red "Exit" sign.

I step outside and close the door quietly behind me. Part of me feels terrible that she's trapped in the building and can't continue to scold me all the way down the alley, but the other part of me is happy to escape the voice of reason.

With my dad's new duties at the railroad and

his hunch about drugs getting stashed in the train cars, I'm sure he's in his office at the train depot comparing manifests with scale receipts to see if the weights check out. I should be able to drive out to the mansion, commandeer the Duncan family watercraft, and check out the first geocache location before anyone misses me.

The large granite stone bearing the Duncan family crest with a large "D" in the center marks my turn. The blur of black-and-white birch trees lining the curving drive is still a little mesmerizing.

I find myself wondering if Ivy was searching Walt's trailer for this list.

The sheer size of the "manse" never ceases to impress. It sits majestically on the shore of the enormous "great lake" that graces the entire region and manages to rival its beauty.

Another random thought interrupts my architectural admiration: Was Walt really cooking meth on a boat?

Two soaring gables sit astride a magnificent entrance, and light spills through massive windows. The entire home is faced in split rock, and at least three chimneys poke through the steeply sloped roof. A terraced patio hugs the side of the home and works its way toward the surging waves.

I park on the flagstones and hurry up the manicured walkway.

Even though the maid is working today, she has no reason to question my presence at the mansion. I decide to show a hint of personal growth and leave a note for my father on the marble countertop.

Hey Dad,
  Just borrowed the boat for
  a quick errand on the lake.
  I'll be back before dinner.
  Mitzy

Determined to learn from past mistakes, I copy the latitude and longitude of the first stash under my name, just as a precaution. I grab a bottle of water from the fridge, remove a doughnut from the box on the counter, and traipse down to the boathouse.

The keys are in the ignition. I take a deep breath, start the engine, and reverse out of the slip. So far so good. I pull the throttle back and shift into what I hope is "forward."

Using the GPS app on my phone, I set the latitude and longitude of my destination and tap for directions. I push the throttle lever to increase my speed and struggle against the large waves.

The first drop is less than half a mile away, and

the sun shines brightly from a nearly cloudless sky. At least I don't have to worry about getting caught in a rainstorm. Easy peasy, lemon squeezy.

Approaching the dot on my phone, I expect to see some kind of buoy or flotation device marking the location. But even though the map tells me I'm literally on top of the cache, I see nothing.

Come on, Moon, think like a smuggler. A flotation device visible on the surface of the water would be seen by anyone passing by. Granted, it's an enormous lake and it would be a heck of a coincidence for someone to happen upon the stash, but it could happen.

So I would need a marker—that's below the surface!

Gazing down at my mood ring, the image of something shimmering beneath the surface flashes across the cabochon. I search around the boat and find a long handled net, I assume for grabbing fish.

Steering the craft in a circle, I keep my eyes focused on anything beneath the surface. As I widen my arc, a quick flash of silver on the right-hand side catches my eye. I slow the boat to a mere sputter and make another circle.

There it is! I tighten the perimeter.

It takes me a while to figure out how to drop anchor, but eventually I get that sorted out and return my focus to the slippery task of scooping up the shiny float.

Approximately twenty tries later, I finally manage to snag whatever is beneath the shimmering float and hoist it up toward the boat.

A large aluminum hook held aloft by a thick Mylar float. Walt may have been stupid, but he was also a genius. Looks like he even put some kind of beacon on there to assist in locating the caches in inclement weather. Nice touch.

I begin the tedious process of pulling the rope up hand over hand and eventually reach the yellow Pelican case. I'm all too familiar with Pelican cases from my days in film school. All valuable equipment gets stored in Pelican cases. They're nearly indestructible and always watertight.

I set the case on the deck, pop the latches, and gasp at the sheer quantity of what has to be methamphetamine.

Panic grips me. I close the case and scan the horizon in a 360. Okay, looks like the racing heart was all my own doing. There is no imminent threat.

Time to head back. I raise the anchor and am busily cursing the lazy speed of the winch, when approaching sirens echo across the water.

The flashing lights are soon followed by the familiar voice of Captain Truby, blaring across the waves. "This is the United States Coast Guard. Cut your engines and put your hands in the air."

Well, this is awkward.

Captain Truby's Coast Guard cutter approaches mine in a bouncy yet direct route and the two officers on deck manage to keep their extremely large and terrifying guns trained on me.

Their vessel knocks into mine and one of the armed men secures the two boats, while the other keeps his weapon pointed directly at my heart. I believe that's called a "kill shot."

She boards my boat and crosses her arms. Black bloused trousers, a black shirt and cap, and an orange reflective vest have replaced the spiffy uniform she wore to Erick's office. Her mirrored sunglasses bounce back my worried expression, and I imagine that right behind those lenses she's staring straight through me. "Don't I know you?" she asks.

I keep my hands up in the air and reply, "Yes, ma'am. We met in Sheriff Harper's office. I'm Mitzy Moon."

"And why exactly are you pulling up a smuggler's cache of drugs, Miss Moon?"

Wait a second. How does she know what I was pulling up? Maybe that "beacon" is some kind of— Images flash through my mind: half burned papers from the ruined trailer; the carefully written list of latitudes and longitudes; the meticulous printing on the report on Erick's desk.

"Walt didn't make the list! You wrote it. You made the list of geocaching sites and Walt planted the meth. He turned on Ivy. He was a snitch." In my mind, the hero's theme music swells.

"That's enough, Moon." Without turning toward her men, she commands, "Take her into custody."

The two armed officers board my vessel. One places me in the all-too-familiar handcuffs and hustles me back onto the Coast Guard vessel. The other officer takes possession of my dad's boat. Boy, am I going to have some explaining to do.

Our caravan of two makes a hasty return to the marina outside the Coast Guard office in Pin Cherry Harbor.

CHAPTER 21

THE SPARTAN COAST GUARD office is almost as no nonsense as its leader Captain Truby. She ushers me to an uncomfortable-looking metal chair and pushes me into it without any of the niceties I've come to expect at the local sheriff's station.

"Please state your full, legal name for the record."

This is going to hurt her more than it hurts me. "Mizithra Achelois Moon."

She hesitates a moment and taps her pen on the table. "Spell it."

"You can call me Mitzy," I offer, before I painstakingly enunciate each letter of my mouthful of a name.

"When did you become involved in the drug trade in Pin Cherry Harbor, Mitzy?"

I have half a mind to tell this woman how incredibly rude I find that insinuation, but somehow I manage to hold my tongue. "I'm not involved in the drug trade. I was following up on a lead."

Captain Truby's humorless laugh echoes off the cold linoleum. "That's the first time a drug trafficker has used that particular line." She rolls her eyes at the armed officer standing in front of the door.

At this point, it seems painfully obvious that she knows nothing of my family standing in the community, or my recent inheritance. She actually believes I'm some kind of drug dealer. I feel it's in my best interest to dispossess her of this notion as quickly as possible. "First of all, Captain Truby, I am the heir to the Duncan fortune. It seems unlikely that I would deal drugs as a side hustle. And second of all, I was investigating Walt Johnson's murder. I stumbled across a clue that was clearly overlooked by the local constabulary." I attempt to lean back smugly, but my handcuffed wrists pinch against the hard metal bar of the chair. I'm forced to hunch forward meekly.

"I'm not sure if calling out your relation to local ex-con Jacob Duncan is your best defense, Miss." She leans back. "He's the only Duncan left, isn't he?"

The snipe at my deceased grandmother and my murdered grandfather hits below the belt, but I'm not about to let it show. It looks like convincing her is going to require a bit of muscle. "Can someone remove my phone from my back pocket?"

She nods to the other officer and he steps forward. "Do you have anything sharp in your pocket? Is there anything in there that's going to hurt me?" His tone is firm, no-nonsense.

"Just my phone." I recall my banter with Gary just before I was kidnapped and add, "It's not a dangerous phone."

He pushes me forward with one hand and extracts my cell phone, laying it on the table in front of his commanding officer.

"Look at the most recent images," I say.

She taps the home button. "It's locked."

"1234," I blurt.

Captain Truby shakes her head and taps in the code.

She doesn't say anything, but even her tightly controlled facial expressions can't hide what she's feeling. My extra sensory perception picks up on a bit of shock, and possibly a hint of guilt. "As you can see, Captain, that's your writing on that piece of paper. I discovered it hidden in the back of a painting, which came from the Walleye Inn. Once I realized those were GPS coordinates, I went on a little geocaching hunt. You just happened to find me—as I found it."

"That's an interesting story, Moon. Do you think it will hold up in court?"

The waves of threatening energy rolling off Captain Truby knock my confidence sideways. Something is completely off. She and I both know that it's her writing on that piece of paper.

A terrifying question knifes into my consciousness. If Walt wasn't working with her to set up a sting, what's the other option?

"Throw her in the hold. I'll notify Ivy one of the drops has been compromised. We'll deal with this intruder later."

Oh. That's the other option. Walt *was* the middleman. Captain Truby isn't setting up a sting, Captain Truby's on the take. I'm starting to wish I'd listened more carefully to my dad's lecture.

Rough hands yank me out of the chair and toss me into a claustrophobically small, all-white cell with only a metal bench. Handcuffs and all. Oh, and I voluntarily gave up my phone and my password. Pure genius.

I haven't even had a chance to settle into my pity party before the cell door opens and a familiar shape is shoved through. "Silas?"

CLANG! The metal door slams shut, leaving us to stew in our own juices.

His brown suit looks no more rumpled than usual, and the subtle aroma of pipe tobacco follows him into the cell. "Good afternoon, Miss Moon. The maid found your missive out at the Duncan estate and notified your father. He in turn, telephoned me, and I was in the process of securing a watercraft when I received a call from Sheriff Harper. He had issued a BOLO for you and the vessel. Fortunately, a local fisherman heard the announcement and recognized the *Tax Sea-vasion* as the missing Duncan boat. He was kind enough to inform the sheriff that the Coast Guard had taken it in. I assumed you'd gotten yourself into trouble, as usual." Silas tilts his head and strokes his grey mustache with thumb and forefinger. "I came to offer my assistance." His stooped shoulders and well-worn tweed coat beg to differ.

"Well, as you can see, I have everything under control."

This statement brings a much louder chuckle from my lawyer than anticipated.

I ignore the implication. "Looks like we have some time to kill. What's the deal with Diane? It's just us. You can tell me what's going on, right?"

His jowls brush across his stooped shoulder as he checks to make sure the cell door is closed. "Diane hunted down Ivy several years ago and inadvertently got Walter involved in drug smuggling. She desired a relationship with her mother, but Ivy simply required access to more boats and Walter's permits. He had the freedom to operate his fishing vessels in Canadian waters without the least inconvenience from authorities."

"But why did she have pills?"

"Ay, there's the rub! Diane came to suspect Ivy of blackmailing Captain Truby because of some compromising photos she caught a glimpse of during her travels in Canada. She put two and two together and imagined that if Ivy could obtain the protection of the Coast Guard, she would no longer require Walter's services. Diane offered to sell the pills at school if Ivy promised to protect Walter."

"That didn't pan out." I exhale the weight of my sadness and ask, "Is that why she was returning the pills?"

"That is her story. However, Diane claims Ivy wouldn't accept the return and swears she's innocent of Walter's demise."

A cold sweat beads at my temples, and I wonder if it was blackmail that drove Truby to defile her duty to country, or was she always a rotten apple? "So, if Ivy didn't kill Walt—was it Truby?"

"I fear it was Truby. Perhaps we are nearer to danger than we realize." Silas strokes his mustache thoughtfully.

An involuntary shudder takes me. "This pretty much seems like maximum danger."

"Agreed." Silas nods. "I'm quite sure the authorities aren't looking for a link between Truby and the explosive device recovered from Walter's boat—"

"The list!" The shout draws a scowl and a shushing from Silas.

"I beg your pardon? There's a list?"

"The list of latitudes and longitudes that I found in the painting."

"I fear I'm missing a vital piece of information. To which painting do you refer?"

"It's from the estate-sale stuff, but it went to the pawnshop, not Gershon's. If the site where Walt's boat wreckage was found matches up with one of the locations on the list—we got her!"

"If you say so . . ." Silas harrumphs and paces the two small strides to the door. He peers out the porthole and returns. "Stand up and let me see those handcuffs."

I do as I'm told and lift my wrists as best I can, behind my back, toward Silas.

He places his hands over the metal cuffs, mumbles a short phrase, and the handcuffs drop to the floor.

"Neat trick. Can you please teach me that one?" I'm not too proud to beg.

Silas slowly bends and retrieves the manacles from the floor. "With your propensity for finding yourself in these types of altercations, I do see the benefit. And as we seem to have nothing but the luxury of time on our hands, I believe now is the perfect moment for a lesson."

There's barely room for both of us to sit side by side on the metal bench, but we wedge ourselves in and Silas locks one side of the handcuffs around my right wrist.

"The basis of all alchemical solutions is transmutation. In this situation, the position of the lock must simply be reformed."

I scrunch up my face. "That doesn't make sense."

Silas leans back and grooms his mustache. "Let me think of another example." His eyes slowly slide from side to side as I imagine him searching for relatable parables. "Ah! Imagine you are holding an ice cube in your hand."

"Okay."

"Eventually the heat from your hand melts the ice, correct?"

I exhale. "Yeah, that's heat versus cold. It's not the same thing as locked versus unlocked."

"That is where you're wrong, Mitzy. It is precisely the same. Place your hand over the lock and visualize ice melting."

I do as I'm told, and, as you might expect, nothing happens.

"Your lack of belief directly affects your efficacy." He places my hand over the lock and his milky-blue eyes stare deeply into my disbelieving grey ones. "You can feel the lock. You can feel metal binding against metal. Now begin to soften that metal, feel the metal give way. Feel the lock slipping, feel it release."

The shock of the handcuff dropping into my lap jolts me out of the trance. I was completely under Silas's spell. I could see and feel everything he described, and then the handcuffs came off. It can't be that easy.

"Would you like to try it on your own?"

"Do the Duke Boys like to drive fast?"

His face shows no sign of recognition.

I search my brain for a snappy comeback without a pop-culture reference. Nada. So, I go with, "Yes."

Silas picks up the handcuff and once again locks one side around my wrist. He sits back and gestures for me to proceed.

I place my hand over the cuff, take a deep breath, and close my eyes. I go through the list just as Silas had described. I feel the metal, I feel it binding, I feel it softening, I feel it release. The handcuffs drop!

"I did it!" My whoop of joy is not appreciated.

Silas places a finger to his lips and mustache.

"I did it," I whisper.

"Excellent. Stand up," instructs Silas.

I do as I'm told.

Silas pulls both my arms behind my back and secures the handcuffs over both wrists.

"What are you doing?"

"Some secrets are best kept, Mitzy."

The door to the holding cell opens and Silas hunches over and becomes feebler before my eyes. His hands shake and his voice falters as he asks, "What's going on? I have no idea what's going on."

Captain Truby fills the doorway menacingly and replies, "I'm sorry you got pulled into this, old man, but your client was poking her nose where it didn't belong." She steps out of the way, and her officer enters and grabs both Silas and me by the arms. He drags us out and waits for his next command.

"Take them down to the Duncan boat. We'll toss them overboard out by Leif Erickson's Abyss."

I stifle a gasp as one officer roughly directs us out of the office and down the ramp to the dock while the other keeps his weapon at the ready, in case we get any ideas.

Silas gives me a little wink before he trips and falls on the wooden dock.

The officer drops his hand from my arm to retrieve Silas and, for the second time in as many days, I dive into the icy waters of the greatest of lakes. As soon as the cold knifes into my skin and sucks the breath from my lungs, I regret my genius plan. With freezing water soaking my clothes and pulling me deeper and deeper, I'm having a lot of trouble re-creating the sense of calm that allowed me to release my handcuffs in the tiny cell.

Bullets ricochet off the surface, and one pierces through the water near my head.

I kick my feet and manage to get underneath the dock. My lungs are screaming for air, and my brain refuses to cooperate. I'm fighting my every instinct to kick to the surface and gulp in some air—when an unexpected calm settles over me.

And this is how I go out. I guess I must be dying.

As my heavy, wet clothing drags me down, the handcuffs drop off. I stroke desperately at the water, pulling myself toward the surface. Toward the air I so desperately need. As I surface, a loud splash disturbs the water behind me.

Oh great, one of her henchmen is after me, and I saw Ashton Kutcher in *The Guardian*, so I know these Coast Guard guys can swim like sharks. I paddle hard, down the length of the dock, and tuck between two boats. When I surface to grab another breath of air, sirens pierce my eardrums. Normally the sound of sirens would bring me comfort, but after discovering Captain Truby's dodgy connection to the smugglers, I'm not sure whom to trust.

The rhythmic splashing of a swimmer powering through the water approaches.

I'm shivering uncontrollably now, and only adrenaline pushes me to swing around the boat and head for shore.

There are no more gunshots, so I guess the marksman abandoned his target practice for some old-school Marco Polo.

I'm not normally a strong swimmer, but the terror surging through my veins gives me a determination I never thought possible. My knee scrapes across some rocks. Shore! I pop my head above the surface and someone shouts, "Get down!"

With no way of knowing whether the command is meant for me or someone else, I submerge my unwilling body into the icy liquid.

A single shot fires.

Am I hit? I can't be sure if the lack of feeling is shock or just the numbing cold.

Strong hands grab me and drag me to the rocky beach.

This is it. This is what my father warned me about. This is what I get for sticking my nose into other people's business.

"Mitzy? Miss Moon? Can you hear me?"

That voice . . . I recognize that voice.

A hand slips under my neck and tilts my head back, while a stubbly cheek brushes against my lips.

If this is some attempt to finish me off, I don't understand.

Strong fingers pinch my nose, and as I open my eyes, I'm greeted by the parted lips of Sheriff Erick descending toward mine.

I blink rapidly, cough, and wave my hands.

Less than an inch from contact, the sheriff pulls his face away and shouts, "She's all right!"

I make an effort to sit, but Erick's hand pushes my shoulder down. "Wait for the paramedics, Moon. Your days as a mermaid are over."

His laugh covers the distress in his eyes. If I had waited a half a second more, his lips would've been on mine. Damn these near-death experiences and my over eagerness to live. Next time—

A stretcher scrapes across the rocks, and two strong sets of hands lift me in unison. As the paramedics hoist the stretcher and carry me toward the waiting ambulance, my eyes linger on the enticing vision of Sheriff Erick in his clingy, wet uniform, and his chest heaving a sigh of relief.

You will be mine, Erick. Oh yes, you will.

CHAPTER 22

I'm STUCK in the hospital overnight for "observation," but the only thing I observe is my father's need to stare at me with extreme disappointment and drink endless cups of coffee to stave off sleep.

"Dad, you can go home and get some sleep. I'll be fine. I'm sure Erick rounded up Truby and her goons."

"I'm not leaving this room until Ivy Lapointe is locked up. A woman who corrupts a decorated Coast Guard officer is more dangerous than you can imagine."

Seems like my dad might be underestimating my ability to imagine danger right now. "Can you at least go and check on Silas?"

Jacob reluctantly agrees, but before he makes it

past my hospital bed the door to my room swings open.

"You have a visitor, Miss Moon." The nurse steps aside and in walks my attorney. Apparently, none the worse for the wear, save a light bruise on his left cheek.

"I realize greeting the sunrise is not your custom, but I managed to convince Odell that you were in desperate need of proper sustenance. He's agreed to open thirty minutes early. Would you and Jacob care to break your fast with me?"

By the time I convince my father, two nurses, and one doctor that I'm perfectly fine, the half hour has passed, and we arrive at Myrtle's Diner along with the rest of the early risers.

Jacob pauses with his hand on the door. "You guys head in. I'm going to have a word with Sheriff Harper."

"Go easy on him, Dad. He got there as fast as he could. Plus, I think he shot a guy for me." I smile and blush with admiration.

Jacob scowls. "Order me a special. I won't be long."

Silas Willoughby and I instantly become small-town heroes. But you know me, I would never let that go to my head. We simply slip into a booth in the diner and nurse our bumps and bruises with strong cups of coffee and, of course, large slices of pin cherry pie, *à la mode*. The new breakfast of champions.

A strange man approaches our table and lays a business card in front of me.

"We will not be granting any interviews," says Silas.

Without a glance at the card, I know this is no reporter. Expensive haircut. Tailored suit. Manicured hands. And his shoes— Wait! I've seen those shoes. I pick up the card. Rory Bombay, Proprietor, Bombay Antiquities and Artifacts.

"Perhaps you were acquainted with the previous owner, a Mr. Gershon?"

I gaze up from the card. I can't be bothered to close my slack mouth. Those green eyes and that hint of stubble . . . He was in my Rare Books Loft. The thought of him being so close to my apartment —to my bed . . . I'm not sure if I'm turned on or terrified.

"Silas Willoughby. I'm Miss Moon's solicitor." Silas shakes the man's hand. "So nice to make your acquaintance. How can I be of assistance?"

Without taking his eyes off me, Rory replies, "Miss Moon has a book in her collection that I am most anxious to purchase."

A strange feeling slithers across the table. My attention shifts from the dreamy dealer to Silas.

He's putting up defenses. He's anxious. He's—he's effectively shut me out. "What's going on?"

Silas reaches across the table, picks up the card, and slides it into his breast pocket. "I will telephone you on Monday to discuss the particulars. To which book do you refer?"

Mr. Bombay's eyes never leave my face, but something sparks deep within the emerald pools when he utters the title. "*Saducismus Triumphatus.*"

Silas rises from the booth and swells with power. "Monday, Mr. Bombay. Good day."

The mysterious gentleman smiles and turns to leave. He places a hand on my shoulder and adds, "I'll look forward to it."

My skin tingles and blood surges to my face. "That man has magic fingers," I whisper.

"Precisely my concern," mumbles Silas.

My eyes widen with shock, but I don't have time for a follow up.

Tally sashays over to the table. "Either of you need a hotter upper?"

I slide my cup of coffee to the end of the table and Tally expertly fills it within a hair's breadth of the top, never spilling a drop.

"Thanks, Tally."

"Any time, superstar." She winks and hustles off

to attend to the other diners in the unusually crowded cafe.

Silas chuckles, wipes a bit of ice cream from his bushy mustache, and changes the subject. "You did quite well with your seaside performance. I was unsure if you would comprehend my meaning, but I was much pleased when you took advantage of my feeble old stumble and dove to freedom." He smiles like a proud father.

I swallow my delicious mouthful of pie before I ask, "What if I hadn't gotten the message? Did you have a backup plan?"

Silas exhales and pats his belly full of pie. "I prefer to focus on the success, rather than the what ifs."

I wonder if he would have taken a bullet for me? Or if he has some power that he planned to use, but didn't have to. Either way, I guess I should listen to his wise words and simply celebrate the victory.

Sitting with my back to the door, I hear it open but it's the grin on my mentor's face that gives away the identity of our guest. I twist in my seat, eager to fill my senses with a slice of sexy sheriff, but I'm crestfallen to note that yesterday's deliciously clingy uniform has been replaced with a completely dry and pressed set. How rude.

"If it isn't our local hero, Mitzy Moon. Jacob said I could find you here."

Several heads in the diner nod their agreement, and two gentlemen raise coffee cups in a toast to my celebrity status.

The sheriff chuckles as he approaches the table. "He's filling out some paperwork. Could be awhile. He said not to wait."

"Eighty-six the special, Odell," I call across the diner.

He tosses me a metal-spatula salute through the orders-up window.

"Do you already have a new case for me?"

"Not today, Moon. I'm here to inform you that even heroes have to make official statements."

Boy, this guy is all business all the time. Maybe I'm wasting my fantasy life on dreams of him letting down his guard and whispering sweet nothings in my ear. Maybe I should spend that energy on a little fantasizing about Rory—

Silas clears his throat loudly.

Once again, I've let my inner delights display themselves on my face. I can almost see the twinkle in my own eyes. "Of course, Erick. Silas and I will come down to the station as soon as we finish our pie."

Erick taps his fingers on the table, nods, and as he leaves, tosses this gem in my direction. "So I'll see you in less than two minutes?" The door closes and mercifully muffles his laughter.

"Your reputation precedes you." Silas gives me an overly formal nod and savors his final bite of pie.

As predicted, my celebratory meal rapidly disappears.

Tally clears our plates, offers more coffee, which we decline, and Silas hands me a napkin.

As evidence of my extreme personal growth, I accept the napkin. Look what a protégé I'm turning out to be.

Odell Johnson makes his way out of the kitchen toward our table.

"Hey, Odell, that was some real fine pie."

He nods his agreement. "I just wanted to thank you for doing right by Walt. You and I both know Diane only got wrapped up in all of this to try to get him squared away. He might not've always made the smartest choices, but he was a good dad." Odell sniffles, wipes his nose with the back of his hand, and says, "Must be allergies."

I smile warmly. "Yeah, I hear they're real bad this fall."

He nods. "Diane's gonna testify against Ivy. She feels terrible about Lars Gershon—Diane does, not Ivy. She let it slip to Ivy about the estate sale before the fire and the DA figures that's when Ivy went lookin' for that fancy painting. She had no idea Walt had stashed it with the pawnshop guy. Poor

Lars. He woulda had no idea what Psycho Ivy was after."

Silas mumbles something under his breath that sounds a little like, "Ah, that was the moniker." But I'm not entirely sure what a moniker is, so I turn my attention back to Odell.

He continues, "Sounds like the DA will drop Diane's charge to a misdemeanor for her cooperation, and he's gonna let her off with some community service. It could've been much worse if you hadn't uncovered that whole conspiracy. I still can't believe Captain Truby let herself be taken in by that good-for-nothin' Ivy. Truby's father must be turning over in his grave. He was a decent man. Made a lot of sacrifices for those kids. At least Junior turned out all right."

Junior must be the younger brother that served in Afghanistan with Erick. I don't bother asking. The details aren't important. What's important is to let Odell thank me profusely in his own quiet, convoluted way.

Silas slides out of the booth and lays a few bills on the table. He places a hand on Odell's shoulder and says, "And you are also a man of fine character, Odell." He walks toward the door and calls back to me, "I'll see you at the station, Mitzy."

Odell chuckles. "If you're not careful, they'll start charging you rent down there." His belly laugh fills the diner and a little tear wets the corner of his eye.

Laughing along, I salute Odell as I leave. He was the first friend I ever made when I came to Pin Cherry Harbor. Maybe I'm not such a bad judge of character after all. Who knows, my luck with men might be about to change.

End of Book 2

But, the mysteries continue...
Curl up with the next book in the Mitzy Moon
Mysteries series!

A NOTE FROM TRIXIE

Another case solved! I'll keep writing them if you keep reading . . .

One of my favorite parts of bringing Mitzy to life has been the wonderful feedback from my early readers. Thank you to my alpha readers Angel, Michael, and Andrew. HUGE thanks to my fantastic beta readers who gave me extremely useful and honest feedback: Veronica McIntyre, Renee Arthur, and Nadine Peterse-Vrijhof. And big hugs to the world's best ARC Team – Trixie's Mystery ARC Detectives!

Three cheers for my brilliant editor Philip Newey! Any remaining errors are my own.

Google can give an author all kinds of helpful information, but there is absolutely no substitute for "straight from the horse's mouth." Thanks to my "horses!" Morgan, thank you for getting me squared away on Odell's Army backstory. Kylie, thank you for answering my foolish questions about tattoos and for coining the phrase "tattoo inception!" And finally, thank you to Josh for all the years you begged for a caracal! I was never as brave as Grams, but your passion for them sent me down the "rabbit hole" and once I learned all I could about the little beasts—I knew I had to have one—even if it lives only in my mind.

Now I'm writing book four in the Mitzy Moon Mysteries series, and I think I may just live in Pin Cherry Harbor forever. Mitzy, Grams, and Pyewacket got into plenty of trouble in book one, *Fries and Alibis*. But I'd have to say that book three, *Wings and Broken Things*, is when most readers say the series becomes unputdownable.

I hope you'll continue to hang out with us.

Trixie Silvertale (November 2019)

WINGS AND BROKEN THINGS

Mitzy Moon Mysteries No. 3

A crime with no eyewitness. A determined psychic sleuth. Will her search for clues take her where angels fear to tread?

Mitzy Moon is eager to test her expanding abilities. While she'd love to look into the hit-and-run that struck down her favorite veterinarian, leads are slim to none. But before she can suss out a single tip, the advances of a charming green-eyed stranger offer a dangerous distraction...

Desperate to put her investigation back on track, she goes undercover at the high school and lands on the wrong side of the law by lunch. And her "get out of jail free card" comes with the help of her meddling Grams, an interfering feline, and her alchemically inclined attorney. But when a curse puts her powers on the fritz, she may not be able to save everyone...

Can Mitzy juggle dating and sleuthing, or will a hex knock off more than her halo?

Wings and Broken Things is the third book in the hilarious paranormal cozy mystery series, Mitzy Moon Mysteries. If you like snarky heroines, supernatural misfits, and a dash of romance, then you'll love Trixie Silvertale's twisty whodunits.

Buy *Wings and Broken Things* to solve a merciful mystery today!

Grab yours here!
readerlinks.com/l/5211997

Scan this QR Code with the camera on your phone. You'll be taken right to the next case!

Come visit Pin Cherry Harbor!

Get access to the Exclusive Mitzy Moon Mysteries character quiz – free!

Find out which character you are in Pin Cherry Harbor and see if you have what it takes to be part of Mitzy's gang.

This quiz is only available to members of the Paranormal Cozy Club, Trixie Silvertale's reader group.

Visit the link below to join the club and get access to the quiz:

Join Trixie's Club
https://trixiesilvertale.com/paranormal-cozy-club/

Once you're in the Club, you'll also be the first to receive updates from Pin Cherry Harbor and access to giveaways, new release announcements, short stories, behind-the-scenes secrets, and much more!

Scan this QR Code with the camera on your phone. You'll be taken right to the page to join the Club!

THANK YOU!

Trying out a new book is always a risk and I'm thankful that you rolled the dice with Mitzy Moon. If you loved the book, the sweetest thing you can do (*even sweeter than pin cherry pie à la mode*) is to leave a review so that other readers will take a chance on Mitzy and the gang.

Don't feel you have to write a book report. A brief comment like, "Can't wait to read the next book in this series!" will help potential readers make their choice.

★★★★★

Leave a quick review here:

https://readerlinks.com/l/792154

★★★★★

Thank you kindly, and I'll see you in Pin Cherry Harbor!

Dangers and Empty Mangers

Heists and Poltergeists

Blades and Bridesmaids

Scones and Tombstones

Vandals and Yule Scandals

Harper and Moon Investigations
Paranormal Cozy Mysteries

Ropes and Last Hopes

Bells and Bombshells

Rodeo Clowns and Shakedowns

Stiffs and Petroglyphs

Fatal Wines and Valentines

April Curses and May Hearses

Wheels and Dirty Deals

Scripts and Empty Crypts

Christmas Catastrophe Mysteries
Culinary Cozy Mysteries

Peppermint Cookie Murder

Apple Dumpling Murder

Linzer Cookie Murder

Chocolate Crinkle Cookie Murder

...more to come!

MAGICAL RENAISSANCE FAIRE MYSTERIES

Explore the world of Coriander the Conjurer. A fortune-telling fairy with a heart of gold!

Book 1:

All Swell That Ends Spell – A dubious festival. A fatal swim. Can this fortune-telling fairy herald the true killer?

Book 2:

Fairy Wives of Windsor – A jolly Faire. A shocking murder. Can this furtive fairy outsmart the killer?

Book 3:

Double Double Royal Trouble – When a treat-peddling witch is found dead, will this cursed faire crumble?

Join Sydney Coleman and her unruly ghosts, as they solve mysteries in a truly haunted mansion!

Book 1: ***Moonlight and Mischief*** – She's desperate for a fresh start, but is a mansion on sale too good to be true?

Book 2: ***Moonlight and Magic*** – A haunted Halloween tour seem like the perfect plan, until there's murder...

Book 3: ***Moonlight and Mayhem*** – An unwelcome visitor. A surprising past. Will her fire sale end in smoke?

ABOUT THE AUTHOR

USA TODAY Bestselling author Trixie Silvertale grew up reading an endless supply of Lilian Jackson Braun, Hardy Boys, and Nancy Drew novels. She loves the amateur sleuths in cozy mysteries and obsesses about all things paranormal. Those two passions unite in all her cozy mysteries, and she's thrilled to write them and share them with you.

When she's not consumed by writing, she bakes to fuel her creative engine and pulls weeds in her herb garden to clear her head (*and sometimes she pulls out her hair, but mostly weeds*).

Greetings are welcome:
trixie@trixiesilvertale.com

f facebook.com/TrixieSilvertale

instagram.com/trixiesilvertale

BB bookbub.com/authors/trixie-silvertale

www.ingramcontent.com/pod-product-compliance
Lightning Source LLC
Chambersburg PA
CBHW030036180626
46810CB00001B/393